DOVER·THRIFT·EDITIONS

Chelkash
and Other Stories

MAXIM GORKY

DOVER PUBLICATIONS, INC.
Mineola, New York

DOVER THRIFT EDITIONS

GENERAL EDITOR: PAUL NEGRI
EDITOR OF THIS VOLUME: SUSAN L. RATTINER

Published in Canada by General Publishing Company, Ltd., 30 Lesmill Road, Don Mills, Toronto, Ontario.
Published in the United Kingdom by Constable and Company, Ltd., 3 The Lanchesters, 162–164 Fulham Palace Road, London W6 9ER.

Bibliographical Note

This Dover edition, first published in 1999, is a republication of three short stories from a standard edition: *Chelkash* (translated by J. Fineberg), *Makar Chudra* (translated by B. Isaacs), and *Twenty-six Men and a Girl* (translated by B. Isaacs).

Library of Congress Cataloging-in-Publication Data

Gorky, Maksim, 1868–1936.
    [Short stories. English. Selections]
    Chelkash and other stories / Maxim Gorky.
        p.   cm. — (Dover thrift editions)
    Contents: Chelkash—Makar Chudra—Twenty-six men and a girl.
    ISBN 0-486-40652-0 (pbk.)
    1. Gorky, Maksim, 1868–1936—Translations into English. I. Title. II. Series.
PG3463.A15   1999
891.73'3—dc21
                                        98-52058
                                               CIP

Manufactured in the United States of America
Dover Publications, Inc., 31 East 2nd Street, Mineola, N.Y. 11501

Note

RUSSIAN WRITER Maxim Gorky (1868–1936), the nom de plume of Aleksey Maksimovich Peshkov, was born in Nizhni-Novgorod (later renamed Gorky in his honor). Recognized as one of the foremost leaders in the Socialist Realism movement, a doctrine encouraging a Socialist view of society in works of art, music, and literature, Gorky was also actively involved in the 1917 Russian Revolution. Gorky identified with the Russian poor, and the protagonists of his stories were typically criminals, ordinary merchants, or laborers. A champion for the downtrodden, Gorky is deemed to be among the greats of Russian literature.

After his father died when he was just five years old, Gorky went to live with his maternal grandfather, who treated him harshly. The budding proletarian author began to earn his own way at the age of nine, assuming a wide variety of odd jobs that drew his attention to working class struggles. His early short stories such as "Makar Chudra" (1892) and "Chelkash" (1895) were first published in Soviet journals. *Sketches and Stories* (1898), his first collection, met with unparalleled success. In "Twenty-six Men and a Girl"—often regarded as his best short story—Gorky describes the lives of bakery workers in an evocative and powerful style that quickly gained popular approval. Securing him an international reputation, these authentic portrayals of social outcasts as also seen in his drama, *The Lower Depths* (1902), and his novel, *Mother* (1907), exerted considerable influence in post-revolutionary Russian society.

Gorky's political activism caused him continual troubles with the tsarist government. A supporter of the Bolsheviks, he was exiled in 1902 for organizing an underground press. The following year, Gorky was elected to the Academy of Sciences, but this honor was rescinded by the government. In 1905, when Gorky was arrested for revolutionary activities, his followers issued formal protests to the tsar on his behalf. He traveled to the United States in 1906 to raise money for the revolution. Gorky returned to Russia after being granted amnesty in 1913.

Among Gorky's greatest achievements were his memoirs. In 1913, he wrote *My Childhood,* the first work in a trilogy of autobiographies that included *In the World* (1915), and *My Universities* (1922). During the 1920s, he published his reminiscences of fellow Russian writers Chekhov, Tolstoy, and Andreyev. Other works by Gorky include several novels, short stories, nonfiction, and plays such as *The Petty Bourgeois* (1901). Ill for many years with recurring tuberculosis, Gorky died in Moscow in 1936.

Contents

CHELKASH

THE BLUE southern sky, darkened by dust, bore a leaden hue; the hot sun, looking down onto the greenish sea as if through a fine grey veil, was barely reflected in the water, which was chopped by the strokes of boats' oars, ships' propellers, the sharp keels of Turkish feluccas and of other vessels that ploughed backwards and forwards in the congested port. The granite-fettered waves, borne down by the immense weights that glided over their crests, beat against the ships' sides and against the shore, growling and foaming, befouled with all sorts of junk.

The clang of anchor chains, the clash of the buffers of the railway cars that were bringing up freight, the metallic wail of iron sheets slipping onto the cobble-stones, the muted sounds of wood striking wood, of rambling carts, of ships' sirens rising to a shrill, piercing shriek and dropping to a muffled roar, and the loud voices of the dock labourers, the seamen and the military Customs guards—all mingled in the deafening music of the working day, and quivering and undulating, hovered low in the sky over the port. And from the land, rising to meet them, came wave after wave of other sounds, now muffled and rumbling, causing everything around to vibrate, and now shrill and shrieking, rending the dusty, sultry air.

The granite, the iron, the timber, the cobble-stones in the port, the ships and the men, all breathed the mighty sounds of this fervent hymn to Mercury. But the human voices, scarcely audible in this tumult, were feeble and comical; and the very men who had originally produced these mighty sounds were comical and pitiful to look at. Their grimy, ragged, nimble bodies, bent under the weight of the merchandise they carried on their backs, flitted to and fro amidst clouds of dust and a welter of heat and sound. They looked insignificant compared with the steel giants, the mountains of merchandise, the rattling railway cars and everything else around them which they themselves had created. The things they themselves had created had enslaved them and robbed them of their personality.

1

The giant steamers, lying with steam up, shrieked and hissed and heaved deep sighs; and every sound they emitted seemed to breathe scorn and contempt for the grey, dusty, human figures that were creeping along their decks, filling the deep holds with the products of their slavish labour. The long files of dock labourers carrying on their backs hundreds of tons of grain to fill the iron bellies of the ships in order that they themselves might earn a few pounds of this grain to fill their own stomachs, looked so droll that they brought tears to one's eyes. The contrast between these tattered, perspiring men, benumbed with weariness, turmoil and heat, and the mighty machines glistening in the sun, the machines which these very men had made, and which, after all is said and done, were set in motion not by steam, but by the blood and sinew of those who had created them—this contrast constituted an entire poem of cruel irony.

The overwhelming noise, the dust which irritated one's nostrils and blinded one's eyes, the baking and exhausting heat, and everything else around, created an atmosphere of tense impatience that was ready to burst out in a terrific upheaval, an explosion that would clear the air and make it possible to breathe freely and easily—after which silence would reign over the earth, and this dusty, deafening, irritating and infuriating tumult would pass away, and the town, the sea and the sky would be tranquil, serene and magnificent. . . .

A bell struck twelve in slow regular strokes. When the last brassy vibrations died away, the savage music of labour sounded softer and a moment later sank to a muffled, discontented murmur. Human voices and the splash of the sea became more audible. It was dinner time.

I

When the dock labourers stopped work and scattered over the port in noisy chattering groups to buy the victuals that the market women were selling, and had squatted down on the cobble-stones in shady corners to eat their dinner, Grishka Chelkash turned up, an old timer, well-known to the people in the port, a confirmed drunkard, and a skilful, daring thief. He was barefooted; his legs were encased in a pair of threadbare corduroy trousers; he wore no hat, and his dirty cotton blouse with a torn collar, which exposed the brown skin drawn tightly over his lean collar bones. His matted, black, grey-streaked hair and his sharp crinkled, rapacious face showed that he had only just got up from sleep. A straw was entangled in his brown moustache, another was sticking to the bristle on his left cheek, and he had a freshly plucked linden twig stuck behind one ear. Tall, gaunt, slightly round-shouldered, he strode slowly over the cobble-stones, wrinkling his hawk-like nose and casting his keen, grey, flashing eyes around, looking for somebody among the dock labourers. Now and again his long, thick, brown moustache twitched like the whiskers of a cat, and his hands, held behind his back, rubbed against each other, while his long, crooked, grasping fingers nervously intertwined. Even here, among the hundreds of rough hoboes like himself, he at once became conspicuous by his resemblance to the hawk of the steppe, by his rapacious leanness, and by his deliberate gait, outwardly calm and even, but internally agitated and alert, like the flight of the bird of prey that he reminded one of.

When he drew level with a group of bare-footed dockers who were sitting in the shade of a pile of coal-laden baskets, a thickset lad, whose stupid face was disfigured by scarlet blotches and his neck badly scratched—evidently the results of a recent scrap—got up to meet him. Walking by the side of Chelkash, he said in an undertone:

"The sailors are missing two bales of cloth. . . . They're searching for them."

"Well?" asked Chelkash, looking the lad up and down.

"What do you mean, well? I say they are searching for them. That's all."

"What? Have they been asking for me to go and help in the search?"

Chelkash smiled and looked in the direction of the warehouse of the Volunteer Fleet.*

"Go to hell!"

The lad turned to go back, but Chelkash stopped him with the exclamation:

"Hey! You do look a sight! Who messed up your shop front like this?" And then he enquired: "Have you seen Mishka about here anywhere?"

"Haven't seen him for a long time!" retorted the other, leaving Chelkash to rejoin his mates.

Chelkash proceeded on his way, greeted by everybody as an old acquaintance; but today he was obviously out of sorts, and instead of replying with his customary banter, he snarled in answer to the questions put to him.

Suddenly a Customs guard appeared from behind a pile of merchandise, a dark-green, dusty, and truculently erect figure. He stood in front of Chelkash, defiantly barring his way, clutched the hilt of his dirk with his left hand and put out his right to take Chelkash by the collar.

---

*A merchant shipping company. — *Trans.*

"Halt! Where are you going?" he demanded.

Chelkash stepped back a pace, raised his eyes to the guard's good-natured but shrewd face and smiled drily.

The Customs guard tried to pull a stern face; he puffed out his round, red cheeks, twitched his brows and rolled his eyes ferociously, but he succeeded only in looking comical.

"How many times have I told you not to go prowling around these docks. I said I'd smash your ribs in if I caught you! But here you are again!" he shouted.

"How do you do, Semyonich! We haven't met for a long time!" Chelkash answered serenely, proferring his hand.

"It wouldn't break my heart if I didn't see you for a century! Clear out of here!"

Nevertheless, Semyonich shook the proferred hand.

"Tell me," continued Chelkash, retaining Semyonich's hand in his tenacious fingers and familiarly shaking his hand. "Have you seen Mishka anywhere around here?"

"Who's Mishka? I don't know any Mishka! You'd better clear out, brother, or else the warehouse guard will see you, and he'll. . . ."

"That red-haired chap I worked with on the *Kostroma* last time," persisted Chelkash.

"The one you go thieving together, you mean, don't you? They took that Mishka of yours to the hospital. He met with an accident and broke his leg. Now go along, brother, while I'm asking you quietly, otherwise I'll give you one in the neck!"

"There! And you say you don't know Mishka! You do know him after all! What are you so wild about, Semyonich?"

"Now then, now then! Don't try to get round me! Clear out of here, I tell you!"

The guard was getting angry, and looking round from one side to another, he tried to tear his hand out of Chelkash's close grip. But Chelkash calmly gazed at the guard from under his thick eyebrows and keeping a tight hold on his hand went on to say:

"Don't hustle me! I'll have my say and then go away. Well now, tell me, how're you getting on? How's the wife, and the children? Are they well?" With flashing eyes, and teeth bared in an ironic smile, he added: "I've been wanting to pay you a visit for a long time, but I've been too busy . . . drinking. . . ."

"Now, now! None of that! None of your jokes, you skinny devil! I'll give it to you hot if you don't look out! . . . What! Do you intend to go robbing in the streets and houses now?"

"Whatever for? There's plenty of stuff lying about here. Plenty I tell you, Semyonich! I hear you've swiped another two bales of cloth! Take care, Semyonich! See you don't get caught!"

Semyonich trembled with indignation, foamed at the mouth, and tried to say something. Chelkash released his hand and calmly made for the dark gates in long, regular strides. The guard kept close on his heels, swearing like a trooper.

Chelkash brightened up and whistled a merry tune through his teeth. With his hands in his trouser pockets he strode along unhurriedly, throwing biting quips and jests to right and left and getting paid in his own coin.

"Hey, Grishka! Look how the bosses are taking care of you!" shouted a dock labourer from a crowd of men who were sprawling on the ground, resting after dinner.

"I've no boots on, so Semyonich is seeing that I don't step onto something sharp and hurt my foot," answered Chelkash.

They reached the gates. Two soldiers ran their hands down Chelkash's clothes and then gently pushed him into the street.

Chelkash crossed the road and sat down on the curbstone opposite a tavern. A file of loaded carts came rattling out of the dock gates. Another, of empty carts, came from the opposite direction, their drivers bumping on the seats. The docks belched forth a howling thunder and clouds of biting dust. . . .

Chelkash felt in his element amidst this frenzied bustle. Solid gains, requiring little labour but much skill, smiled in prospect for him. He was confident of his skill, and wrinkling his eyes he pictured to himself the spree he would have next morning when his pockets were filled with bank notes. . . . He thought of his chum, Mishka; he would have been very useful to him that night if he had not broken his leg. He swore to himself as doubt crossed his mind as to whether he would be able to manage alone, without Mishka. He wondered what the weather would be like at night, and looked at the sky. He lowered his eyes and glanced down the street.

A half a dozen paces away, on the cobbles, leaning back against the curb, sat a young lad in a coarse blue homespun blouse and trousers of the same material, bast shoes on his feet, and a dilapidated brown cap on his head. Beside him lay a small knapsack and a scythe without a haft, wrapped in straw and carefully tied with string. The lad was broad-shouldered, thickset, fair-haired, and had a sunburnt weather-beaten face and large blue eyes, which looked at Chelkash trustfully and good-naturedly.

Chelkash bared his teeth, poked his tongue out, and pulling a horrible face, stared at the lad with wide-open eyes.

The lad blinked in perplexity at first, but soon he burst out laughing and shouted between his chuckles: "Aren't you funny!" And then, scarcely rising from the ground, he shifted awkwardly over to Chelkash, dragging his knapsack through the dust and rattling the heel of his scythe over the cobble-stones.

"Been on the booze, eh, brother?" he asked Chelkash, tugging at the latter's trousers.

"Yes, baby, something like that!" confessed Chelkash with a smile. He at once took a fancy to this sturdy, good-natured lad with the bright childish eyes. "You've been out haymaking, eh?" he enquired.

"Yes! . . . But it was plenty of work and little pay. I made nothing by it. And the people! Hundreds of them! Those people from the famine districts came pouring in and knocked the price down. The job was hardly worth taking. In the Kuban they paid only sixty kopecks. Something awful! . . . And they say that before they used to pay three, four and five rubles!"

"Before! . . . Before they used to pay three rubles just to look at a Russian! I used to do this job myself about ten years ago. I would go to a stanitsa* and say—I'm a Russian! And they'd look me up and down, feel my arms, shake their heads in wonder and say: 'Here, take three rubles!' And then they'd give you food and drink, and invite you to stay as long as you like!"

The lad listened to what Chelkash was saying with mouth wide open and amazement and admiration written on his round, tanned face; but soon he realized that the hobo was pulling his leg, and, smacking his lips, he burst into a hearty laugh. Chelkash kept a straight face, hiding his smile under his moustache.

"I'm a boob! You talk as if it was all true, and I listen to it and believe it. . . . But, still, so help me God, things were better there before!"

"Well, and what am I saying? Ain't I saying that before things were. . . ."

"Stop kidding!" interrupted the boy with a wave of his hand. "What are you, a shoemaker? Or a tailor? You, I mean."

"Me?" asked Chelkash in his turn, and after thinking for a moment, he said: "I'm a fisherman."

"A fish-er-man! Is that so! So you catch fish?"

"Fish! Why fish? The fishermen here don't only catch fish. Mostly it's drowned bodies, lost anchors, sunken ships—things like that. They have special hooks for this work. . . ."

"Yah! It's all lies! . . . They must be the fishermen they sing about in the song:

*Cossack village.—*Trans.*

*On arid shores
We spread our nets,
And barns and sheds we trawl. . . .*

"Have you ever met fishermen like that?" asked Chelkash with a smile, looking hard at the boy.

"Met them? No, where could I have met them? But I've heard about them. . . ."

"What do you think of them?"

"That kind of fisherman, you mean? Well . . . they're not a bad lot. They're free. They have freedom. . . ."

"What's freedom to you? . . . Do you like freedom?"

"What do you think? Be your own master. Go where you like, do what you like. . . . I should say so! You can keep yourself straight and have no milestone round your neck. Have a good time, and nothing to worry about, except keep God in mind. What could be better?"

Chelkash spat contemptuously and turned his head away.

"With me it's like this," continued the boy. "My father's dead. We've only a patch of a farm. My mother's old. The land's all dried up. What can I do? I've got to live. But how? I don't know. I thinks to myself—I'll go and be a son-in-law in a good house. But what's the use? It would be all right if the father-in-law gave his daughter a share of his property, and we could set up for ourselves. But do you think he'd do that? Not a bit. The devil wants to keep it all for himself and expects me to slave for him . . . for years! You see what I mean? But if I could earn a hundred or a hundred and fifty rubles, I'd be independent, and I'd say to the father-in-law—you can keep your property! If you give Marfa a share, all well and good. But if you don't . . . thank God she's not the only girl in the village! I'd be quite free. On my own. . . . Y-e-s!" The boy heaved a deep sigh and went on to say: "But what can I do now? Nothing. I'll have to go and slave for a father-in-law. I thought I'd go to the Kuban and earn a couple of hundred rubles, and then everything would be all right. I'd be able to live like a gentleman. But I didn't make anything. So I'll have to go as a labourer after all. . . . I'll never have my own farm now! Ah, well!"

It was quite evident that the lad was extremely reluctant to go as a son-in-law, for as he finished speaking his face became beclouded with grief and he squirmed as he lay on the ground.

Chelkash asked him:

"Where are you bound for now?"

"Home, of course! Where else?"

"How do I know? You might be bound for Turkey. . . ."

"T-u-rkey!" drawled the boy in astonishment. "What Christians go to Turkey? That's a nice thing to say!"

"You're a fool!" said Chelkash, heaving a sigh and turning his head away again. This sturdy peasant lad stirred something in him. . . .

He became conscious of a vague, but steadily growing feeling of vexation gnawing at the pit of his stomach which prevented him from concentrating his mind on the task he had before him that night.

Offended by the snub which had just been administered to him, the boy muttered something under his breath and now and again cast a sidelong glance at the hobo. He pouted his lips, puffed out his cheeks, and far too rapidly blinked his eyes in the most comical fashion. He was obviously disappointed at the conversation with this bewhiskered tramp having been brought to such an abrupt close.

But the tramp paid no more attention to him. He sat on the curbstone engrossed in thought, whistling softly to himself, and beating time with his dirty, bare heel.

The lad wanted to pay him out for the snub.

"Hey, fisherman! Do you often go on the booze?" he began, but the "fisherman" suddenly turned his face towards him and asked:

"Listen, baby! Do you want to do a job of work with me tonight? Tell me quick!"

"What kind of job?" the lad asked suspiciously.

"What do you mean, what kind? Any kind I give you. . . . We'll go fishing. You'll row the boat."

"Oh, all right. Not so bad. I don't mind taking a job. But . . . I won't get into trouble with you, will I? You're a dark one. . . . There's no understanding you."

Chelkash again became conscious of a feeling like heartburn rising in his chest. In a low voice of cold anger he said:

"Then don't chatter about what you don't understand. . . . If you're not careful I'll give you a crack over the head that'll make you understand."

His eyes flashed. He jumped up from the curbstone, twirled his moustache with the fingers of his left hand and clenched his right hand into a hard brawny fist.

The boy was frightened. He glanced round rapidly, blinked timidly, and also sprang to his feet. The two stood looking each other up and down in silence.

"Well!" asked Chelkash sternly. He was burning and trembling with rage at the insult he had received from this callow youth whom he had despised when talking to him, but whom he now hated because he had such a healthy, tanned face, bright blue eyes and short sturdy arms, and because he lived in a village somewhere, had a home there, and some rich farmer was asking him to be his son-in-law; because of his whole past and present, but most of all because this lad, who was only a baby compared with himself, dared to love freedom, the value of which he did not appreciate, and which he did not need. It is always unpleasant to see a man whom you regard as being inferior to and lower than yourself love or hate the same things that you love and hate and thereby resemble you.

The lad glared at Chelkash and felt that the latter was his master.

"Oh . . . I don't mind," he said, "I'm looking for a job, ain't I? It's all the same to me who I work for, you or somebody else. All I wanted to say was . . . you don't look like a working man, you're . . . er . . . so ragged. Of course, I know it might happen to anybody. Lord, haven't I seen enough drunkards! Lots of them! And some even worse than you."

"All right, all right! So you agree?" Chelkash interrupted in a milder tone.

"Me? Why, of course! With pleasure! But how much will you pay me?"

"I pay according to results. It depends on the results. . . . On the catch. D'you understand? You might get a fiver. Will that be all right?"

Now that it was a question of money the peasant wanted to be definite, and he wanted his employer to be definite too. Again distrust and suspicion awoke in his mind.

"No, that doesn't suit me, brother!"

Chelkash also began to play the part.

"Don't argue. Wait! Let's go to the pub!" he said.

They walked down the street side by side. Chelkash twirled his moustache with the important air of an employer. The lad's face expressed complete readiness to obey, and at the same time complete distrust and apprehension.

"What's your name?" Chelkash asked him.

"Gavrila," the boy answered.

When they entered the dingy smoke-begrimed tavern, Chelkash walked up to the bar and in the familiar tone of a frequenter ordered a bottle of vodka, some shchi, roast meat, and tea. When all this was served, he curtly said to the barman: "On tick!" The barman silently nodded his head. This scene impressed Gavrila and roused in him a profound respect for this man, his master, who was so well known and enjoyed such credit in spite of his disreputable appearance.

"Well, we'll have a bite now and then talk business. But wait here a moment, I have somewhere to go," said Chelkash.

He went out. Gavrila looked around him. The tavern was in a basement; it was damp and dismal, and a suffocating smell of vodka fumes, stale tobacco smoke, tar, and of some other pungent substance pervaded the place. At a table, opposite Gavrila, sat a red-bearded drunken man in seaman's dress, covered from head to foot with coal dust and tar. Hiccoughing every now and again, he sang a song in twisted and broken words that sometimes sounded like a hiss and sometimes were deeply guttural. He was evidently not a Russian.

Behind him sat two Moldavian women, ragged, black-haired and sunburnt, and they too were drunkenly singing a song.

Out of the gloom other figures emerged, all strangely dishevelled, and half drunk, noisy and restless. . . .

Gavrila began to feel afraid and longed for the return of his master. All the noises of the tavern merged in one monotonous tone, and it seemed as though some enormous beast was growling, as though, possessing hundreds of different voices, it was angrily and blindly struggling to get out of this stone pit, but was unable to find the exit. Gavrila felt as though his body was absorbing something intoxicating and heavy, which made him dizzy and dimmed his eyes, which were roaming round the tavern with curiosity mixed with fear. . . .

Chelkash came back and they began to eat and drink, talking as they proceeded with their meal. After the third glass of vodka, Gavrila was drunk. He felt merry and wanted to say something to please his master, who was such a fine fellow and had given him this splendid treat. But the words which welled up in his throat in waves could not, for some reason, slip off his tongue, which had suddenly become so strangely heavy.

Chelkash looked at him and said with an ironic smile:

"Half seas over already! Ekh, you milksop! What will you be like after the fifth glass? . . . Will you be able to work?"

"Don't . . . be . . . afraid . . . brother," stammered Gavrila. "You'll . . . be . . . satisfied. I love you! Let me kiss you, eh?"

"Now then, none of that! Here, have another drink!"

Gavrila took another drink, and another, until everything around him began to float in even, undulating waves. This made him feel unwell and he wanted to vomit. His face looked foolishly solemn. When he tried to talk he smacked his lips in a comical way and mooed like a cow. Chelkash gazed at him absently, as if recalling something, thoughtfully twirling his moustache and smiling sadly.

The tavern rang with a drunken roar. The red-haired seaman was sleeping with his head resting on his elbows.

"All right, let's go," said Chelkash, getting up from the table.

Gavrila tried to get up too, but could not. He swore, and laughed idiotically as drunken men do.

"What a wash-out!" muttered Chelkash, resuming his seat at the table opposite Gavrila.

Gavrila kept on chuckling and gazing stupidly at his master. The latter stared back at him, keenly and thoughtfully. He saw before him a man whose life had fallen into his wolfish clutches. He felt that this life was in his power to turn in any direction he pleased. He could crumple it like a playing card, or could help place it in a firm peasant groove. He felt that he was the other one's master, but through his mind ran the thought that this lad would never have to drain the cup of bitterness that fate had compelled him, Chelkash, to do. . . . He both envied and pitied this young life, he despised it, and was even conscious of a feeling of regret as he pictured the possibility of it falling into other hands like his own. . . . But in the end all these feelings merged into one that was both paternal and practical. He was sorry for the lad, but he needed him. He took Gavrila under the armpits, lifted him up and gently prodding him from behind with his knee, he pushed him out into the tavern yard, laid him in the shade of a wood-pile, sat down beside him and lit his pipe. Gavrila wriggled about for a while, moaned, and fell asleep.

II

"Are you ready?" Chelkash in an undertone asked Gavrila, who was fumbling with the oars.

"In a minute! This rowlock's loose. Can I give it just one bang with the oar?"

"No! Don't make a sound! Force it down with your hand and it will slip into its place."

Both were noiselessly handling a boat that was moored to the stern of one of a whole flotilla of small sailing barges laden with oak staves, and of large Turkish feluccas laden with palm and sandal wood and thick cyprus logs.

The night was dark. Heavy banks of ragged clouds floated across the sky. The sea was calm. The water, black and thick, like oil, gave off a humid, saline smell and lazily lapped against the ship's sides and the beach, gently rocking Chelkash's boat. Far from the shore loomed the dark hulls of ships, their masts pointing to the sky, tipped with different coloured lights. The sea, reflecting these lights, was dotted with innumerable coloured patches, which shimmered on its soft, black, velvety surface. The sea was sound asleep, like a labourer after a hard day's work.

"We're off!" said Gavrila, dropping his oars into the water.

"Aye, aye!" said Chelkash, pulling hard with his steering oar to bring the boat into the strip of water between the barges. The boat sped swiftly over the slippery water, and with each stroke of the oars the water was lit up with a bluish phosphorescent radiance that trailed like a long, soft, fluttering ribbon from the boat's stern.

"Does your head still ache?" Chelkash asked in a kindly voice.

"Something awful! . . . It's ringing like a bell. . . . I'll splash some water over it in a minute."

"There's no need to do that. Take this. It'll help your inside, and you'll soon get better," said Chelkash, handing Gavrila a flask.

"I doubt it. . . . Well, God bless us. . . ."

A soft gurgling sound was heard.

"Hey, you! That's enough!" said Chelkash, stopping the boy from drinking more.

The boat pushed ahead again, noiselessly and swiftly winding its way among the ships. . . . Suddenly it shot out from among the crowd of ships, and the sea—infinite and mighty—spread out before them into the blue distance, where mountains of clouds towered out of the water—some violet and grey with puffy yellow borders, others greenish, the colour of sea water, and others of a dull, leaden hue, of the kind which throw heavy, mournful shadows. The clouds moved slowly, now merging with and now skirting each other, mingling their colours and forms, absorbing each other and again emerging in new shapes, majestic and frowning. . . . There was something sinister in the slow movement of this soulless mass. It seemed as though over there, on the edge of the sea, their number was infinite, and that they would eternally creep across the sky in this indifferent manner with the malicious object of preventing it from shining again over the slumbering sea with its millions of golden eyes—the multi-coloured stars, living and dreamily radiant, exciting lofty desires in men to whom their pure radiance is precious.

"The sea's fine, isn't it?" asked Chelkash.

"Not bad! Only it makes me feel afraid," answered Gavrila, pulling strongly and steadily at the oars. The water was barely audible as it splashed under the strokes of the long oars and shone with the warm bluish light of phosphorus.

"Afraid! You boob!" exclaimed Chelkash contemptuously.

He, the thief, loved the sea. His vibrating nervous nature, thirsting for impressions, could not contemplate enough the dark, boundless, free and mighty expanse. He felt hurt when he heard this answer to his enquiry about the beauty of the thing he loved. Sitting in the stern, he cleaved the water with his oar and calmly gazed ahead, feeling that he would like to glide far away over its velvety surface.

The sea always gave him a warm expansive feeling which filled his whole soul and purged it somewhat of the dross of everyday life. He appreciated this, and loved to see himself a better man, here, amidst the water and the air, where thoughts of life, and life itself, always lose, the former their painful acuteness, and the latter all value. At night, the sound of the sea's soft breathing as it slept floats evenly over its surface, and this limitless sound fills a man's soul with serenity, and gently subduing its evil impulses rouses in it mighty dreams. . . .

"Where's the tackle?" Gavrila suddenly asked, looking anxiously into the bottom of the boat.

Chelkash started.

"The tackle? I've got it here, in the stern."

He felt ashamed at having to lie to this boy, and he also regretted the thoughts and feelings that had been disturbed by this boy's question. It made him angry. The familiar sense of burning rose in his breast and throat, and this irritated him still more.

"Now look here!" he said to Gavrila in a hard, stern voice. "You sit still and mind your own business. I hired you to row. Do the job I hired you for. If you wag your tongue too much, you'll be sorry for it! Do you understand me?"

The boat shivered for a moment and stopped. The oars remained in the water, causing it to foam. Gavrila wriggled uncomfortably on his seat.

"Row!"

A foul oath shook the air. Gavrila swung back his oars. The boat shot forward, as if with fright, and sped on at a rapid, jerky pace, noisily cleaving the water.

"Steady now, steady!"

Chelkash stood up in the stern, and keeping hold of the steering oar, he glared coldly into Gavrila's pale face. Bending forward, he looked like a cat crouching for a spring. In his rage he ground his teeth so hard that it could be distinctly heard, and Gavrila's teeth, chattering with fear, were no less audible.

"Who's that shouting?" came a stern cry from the sea.

"Row! Row, you devil! . . . Quieter! . . . I'll murder you, you dog! . . . Go on! . . . Row! . . . One! Two! Make a sound, and I'll tear you limb from limb!" hissed Chelkash. And then he went on in a jeering tone: "Afraid! Booby!"

"Mother of God. . . . Holy Mary . . ." whispered Gavrila, trembling with fear and exertion.

The boat swung round smoothly and returned to the docks, where the ship's lights crowded in multi-coloured groups, and the tall masts were visible.

"Hey! Who's that shouting?" came the voice again, but it sounded more distant this time. Chelkash became calmer.

"It's you that's shouting," he said in answer to the distant voice, and then he turned to Gavrila, who was still muttering his prayers, and said: "Well, brother, you're lucky! If that devil had come after us, it would have been all up with you. Do you understand what I mean? I'd have put you over to feed the fishes!"

Chelkash now spoke calmly and even good-humouredly, but Gavrila still trembling with fear, begged of him:

"Let me go! I ask you in the name of Christ, let me go! Put me ashore somewhere! Ay-ay-ay! . . . I'm lost! I'm a lost man! Remember God and let me go! What do you want me for? I'm no good for this sort of job. . . . I've never been on one like this before. . . . This is the first time. . . . Lord! I'm lost. I'm lost! Christ, how you fooled me, brother, eh? It's a sin. . . . You are damning your own soul! . . . Some business. . . ."

"What business?" Chelkash asked sternly. "What business, eh?"

The lad's fear amused him, and he delighted in it as well as in the thought of what a terrible fellow he, Chelkash, was.

"Shady business, brother! . . . Let me go, for God's sake! . . . What do you want me for? . . . Please. . . . Be good. . . ."

"Shut up! If I didn't need you, I wouldn't have taken you. Do you understand? . . . Well, shut up!"

"Lord!" sighed Gavrila.

"Stop snivelling, or you'll get it in the neck!" snapped Chelkash.

But Gavrila, unable to restrain himself any longer, sobbed quietly, wept, sniffed, wriggled on his seat, but rowed strongly, desperately.

The boat shot forward like an arrow. Again the dark hulls of the ships loomed before them, and soon the boat was lost among them, winding like a shuttle in and out of the narrow strips of water between them.

"Now listen! If anybody asks you about anything, you're to keep mum, if you want to keep alive, that is! Do you understand me?"

"Ekh!" sighed Gavrila resignedly in answer to this stern command. Then he added bitterly: "I'm done for, I am!"

"Stop snivelling, I tell you!" said Chelkash in an angry whisper.

This whisper robbed Gavrila of all capacity to think; his mind was benumbed by a chill foreboding of evil. He mechanically dropped the oars, leaned far back, raised the oars and dropped them again, all the time keeping his eyes riveted on the tips of his bast shoes.

The sleepy murmur of the waves sounded angry and terrifying. They entered the docks. . . . From beyond its granite walls came sounds of human voices, the splashing of water, singing and shrill whistling.

"Stop!" whispered Chelkash. "Ship your oars! Hold on to the wall! Quieter, you devil!"

Gavrila clutched at the wall and worked the boat along; the thick

coating of slime that covered the masonry deadened the sound of the
gunwale as it scraped along its side.

"Stop! . . . Give me the oars! Come this way! Where's your passport?
In your knapsack? Give me your knapsack! Look sharp! That's to prevent your running away, my friend. . . . You won't run away now. You
might have bolted without the oars, but you'd be afraid to run away
without your passport. Wait here! Mind! If you blab—I'll find you even
if you're at the bottom of the sea!"

Suddenly clutching at something with his hands, Chelkash leaped
upwards and vanished over the wall.

Gavrila shuddered. . . . All this had happened so quickly. He felt the
accursed burden of fear which weighed upon him in the presence of
this bewhiskered, skinny thief, dropping, slipping off his shoulders. . . .
Here was a chance to get away! . . . He breathed a sigh of relief and
looked around. On the left towered a black, mastless hull; it looked like
an enormous coffin, deserted and empty. . . . Every wave that struck its
side awoke a hollow, muffled echo that sounded like a sigh. On the
right, the grey stone wall of the mole stretched above the surface of the
water, like a cold, heavy serpent. Behind him loomed some black piles,
and in front, in the space between the wall and the coffin, he could see
the sea, silent, desolate, and the black clouds floating above it. The
clouds moved across the sky slowly, large and ponderous, spreading
horror out of the darkness and seeming ready to crush one with their
weight. All was cold, black and sinister. Gavrila grew frightened again,
and this fright was worse than that with which Chelkash imbued him;
it gripped his breast in its powerful embrace, reduced him to a helpless
clod and held him fast to the seat of the boat.

Silence reigned all around. Not a sound was heard, except for the
sighing of the sea. The clouds still crept across the sky slowly and lazily,
but they rose out of the sea in infinite numbers. The sky too looked like
a sea, but a restless one, suspended over the calm, smooth and slumbering sea below. The clouds seemed to be descending upon the earth
in grey, curly waves, into the chasms from which the wind had torn
them, and upon the newly-rising waves, not yet crested with angry
greenish foam.

Gavrila felt crushed by this gloomy silence and beauty and yearned
to see his master again. Suppose he didn't come back? . . . Time passed
slowly, more slowly than the clouds creeping across the sky. . . . And as
time passed the silence became more sinister. . . . At last the sounds of
splashing and rustling and something resembling a whisper came from
the other side of the mole. Gavrila thought he would die on the spot.

"P'st! Are you asleep? Hold this. . . . Careful now!" It was Chelkash's
muffled voice.

Something heavy and cube-shaped dropped from the wall. Gavrila caught it and put it in the bottom of the boat. A second object of the same kind followed. And then Chelkash's tall figure appeared over the wall, the oars appeared out of somewhere, Gavrila's knapsack fell at his feet, and breathing heavily, Chelkash slipped into the stern of the boat.

Gavrila gazed at him with a pleased but timid smile.

"Are you tired?" he asked.

"Yes, a bit! Now then take to the oars and pull! Pull with all your might! You've done well, my lad! Half the job's done. The only thing now is to slip past those devils out there—and then you can get your share and go home to your Masha. I suppose you have a Masha, haven't you?"

"N-no!" answered Gavrila, pulling at the oars with all his might. His chest heaved like a pair of bellows and his arms worked like steel springs. The water swirled from under the boat's keel, and the blue track at its stern was wider now. Gavrila was drenched with his own perspiration, but he continued to row with all his might. Twice that night he had had a terrible fright; he did not wish to have a third one. All he longed for was to get over this accursed job as quickly as possible, to go ashore and run away from this man before he did indeed kill him, or get him landed in jail. He decided not to discuss anything with him, not to contradict him, to do all he told him to do, and if he succeeded in escaping from him, to offer a prayer to St. Nicholas the Miracle-Worker the very next morning. An ardent prayer was ready to burst from his breast at this very moment, but he restrained himself. He puffed like a steam engine and now and again glanced at Chelkash from under his brows.

But Chelkash, tall, thin, his body bent forward, looking like a bird ready to take to flight, peered with hawkish eyes into the darkness ahead and twitched his beaklike nose. He grasped the steering oar tightly with one hand and with the other twirled his moustache, which also twitched from the smiles that twisted his thin lips. He was pleased with his haul, with himself, and with this lad who was so terribly frightened of him, and whom he had converted into his slave. He watched Gavrila putting every ounce of strength into his oars and felt sorry for him. He wanted to cheer him up.

"Hey!" he said softly with a laugh. "You were frightened, weren't you?"

"N-no! Not much," gasped Gavrila.

"You needn't pull so hard now. It's all over. There's only one spot that we've got to pass. . . . Take a rest. . . ."

Gavrila obediently stopped rowing, wiped the perspiration from his face with his sleeve and dropped the oars.

"Well, have another go now," said Chelkash after a little while. "But don't make the water talk. There's a gate we have to pass. Quietly now, quietly! They're a stern lot here. . . . They wouldn't hesitate to shoot and bore a hole in your head before you have time to shout—oh!"

The boat now glided slowly over the water making scarcely a sound, except for the blue drops that dripped from the oars and caused small, blue, momentary patches to form on the water where they fell. The night became darker and even more silent. The sky no longer resembled a storm-tossed sea—the clouds had spread and covered it with a smooth heavy blanket that hung low and motionless over the water. The sea became still calmer and blacker, its warm saline odour became still more pungent, and it no longer seemed as broad as it was before.

"I wish it would rain!" whispered Chelkash. "We'd get through as if we were behind a curtain."

On the right and left eerie structures loomed out of the black water—barges, motionless, gloomy, and also black. But on one of them a light was moving; evidently somebody carrying a lantern was walking on the deck. The sea sounded plaintive and hollow, as it lapped against the sides of the barges, and the barges answered with a cold, muffled echo, as if arguing with the sea and refusing to yield to its plaint.

"A cordon!" exclaimed Chelkash in a scarcely audible whisper.

The moment Chelkash told him to row more slowly, Gavrila was again overcome by that feeling of tense expectation. He bent forward and peered into the darkness, and he felt as if he were growing, as if his bones and sinews were stretching within him, giving him a dull pain; his head, filled with but one thought, ached; the skin on his back quivered, and small, sharp, cold needles were shooting through his legs. His eyes ached from the tenseness with which he peered into the darkness, out of which, every moment, he expected to hear the cry: "Stop, thief!"

And now, when Chelkash whispered "cordon," Gavrila shuddered; a piercing, burning thought shot through his brain and sent his taut nerves tingling. He wanted to shout and call for help. . . . He opened his mouth, rose slightly from the seat, stuck out his chest and took a deep breath—but suddenly he was paralysed by fear, which struck him like a whip. He closed his eyes and collapsed in the bottom of the boat.

Ahead of the boat, far away on the horizon, out of the black water, an enormous, fiery-blue sword rose and cleaved the darkness of the night; it ran its edge over the clouds and then lay on the breast of the sea, a broad blue strip. And within this bright strip ships appeared out of the darkness, ships hitherto invisible, black, silent, and shrouded in the solemn gloom of the night. They looked as though they had long been at the bottom of the sea, sent there by the mighty power of the storm, and had now risen at the command of the fiery sword that was born of the sea—had risen to look at the sky and at everything that was on the water. . . . Their rigging, clinging to their masts like festoons of seaweed brought up from the sea bottom together with the black giants who were enmeshed in their net. The sinister blue sword rose again out of the depth of the sea, and flashing, again cleaved the night, and again lay flat on the water, but in another direction. And where it lay, other ships' hulls, hitherto invisible, appeared.

The boat stopped and rocked on the water as if in perplexity. Gavrila lay in the bottom of the boat, his face covered with his hands. Chelkash jabbed at him with his foot and hissed furiously:

"That's the Customs cruiser, you fool. . . . It's an electric lamp! Get up, you dolt! They'll shine the light on us in a minute and everything will be all up with you and me! Get up!"

At last a kick from the heel of a heavy top boot heavier than the first caught Gavrila in the back. He started up, and still afraid to open his eyes, took his seat, groped for the oars and began to row.

"Quieter! Quieter, or I'll murder you! . . . What a dolt you are, the devil take you! What frightened you, ugly mug? A lantern, that's all it is! Quieter with the oars . . . you sour-faced devil! . . . They're on the lookout for smugglers. They won't see us—they're too far out. Don't be afraid, they won't see us. Now we. . . ." Chelkash looked round triumphantly. "Of course! We're out of it! Phew! . . . Well, you're lucky, you thick-headed boob!"

Gavrila said nothing. He pulled at the oars and, breathing heavily, looked out of the corners of his eyes in the direction where the fiery sword was rising and falling. He could not possibly believe what Chelkash said—that this was only a lantern. The cold blue radiance that cleaved the darkness caused the sea to sparkle with mysterious silvery brilliance, and Gavrila again felt hypnotized by that soul-crushing fear. He rowed mechanically, crouching as if expecting a blow from above, and now he was bereft of all desire—he was empty and soulless. The excitement of this night had driven everything human out of him.

But Chelkash was jubilant. His nerves, accustomed to shocks, were now relaxed. His moustache twitched voluptuously and a light shone in his eyes. He felt splendid. He whistled through his teeth, inhaled deep breaths of the moist sea air. He looked around, and smiled good-naturedly when his eyes fell upon Gavrila.

The wind swept down and chopped up the sea. The clouds were now thinner and less opaque, but they covered the whole sky. The wind, though still light, was freely sweeping over the sea, but the clouds were motionless and seemed to be absorbed in grey, dull thought.

"Now lad, it's time you pulled yourself together! You look as if all your guts have been squeezed out of your body and there's nothing left but a bag of bones! It's all over now. Hey!"

Gavrila was pleased to hear a human voice at last, even if that voice was Chelkash's.

"I can hear what you say," he said softly.

"Very well, then, milksop. . . . Come and steer and I'll take the oars. I suppose you're tired."

Gavrila mechanically changed places with Chelkash, and as they crossed, Chelkash saw the boy's woe-begone face, and he noticed that his legs were trembling. He felt sorry for him. Patting him on the shoulder, he said:

"Come on, lad! Don't be so down in the dumps. You've earned a good bit tonight. I'll reward you well, my boy. Would you like the feel of a twenty-five ruble bill?"

"I don't want anything. All I want is to get ashore. . . ."

Chelkash waved his hand in disgust, spat, took up the oars and began to row, swinging the oars far back with his long arms.

The sea woke up and began to play with its little waves, giving birth to them, ornamenting them with fringes of foam, dashing them against each other, and breaking them up into fine spray. The foam melted with hisses and sighs, and the air all around was filled with a musical splashing noise. Even the darkness seemed to come to life.

Chelkash began to talk.

"Well now, tell me," he said. "You'll go back to your village and get married, and start grubbing the earth and sow corn. The wife will start bearing children. You won't have enough food for them. Well, you'll be struggling all your life. . . . Is there any pleasure in that?"

"Pleasure! I should say there isn't!" answered Gavrila with a shudder.

Here and there the wind rent the clouds apart and scraps of the sky with one or two stars in them peeped between the spaces. Reflected in the sea, these stars played among the waves, now vanishing and now twinkling again.

"Steer to the right!" said Chelkash, "we shall be there soon. . . . Y-e-ss! . . . We're finished. It was a nice job! D'you see how it is? . . . One night's work, and we land a cool five hundred!"

"Fi-v-e hundred?!" drawled Gavrila incredulously. But he at once caught fright and hurriedly asked, kicking one of the bales at the bottom of the boat: "What's this?"

"That's worth a lot of money. If we sold it at its proper price we could get a thousand for it. But I'll ask for less. . . . Clever, ain't it?"

"Y-e-s?" drawled Gavrila interrogatively. "I wish I could get a bag like that!" he added with a sigh as he suddenly remembered his village, his wretched farm, his mother, and all that was distant and dear to him, and for the sake of which he had left home to earn some money, and had gone through all the horrors of this night. He was overwhelmed by a wave of recollections of his little village which scrambled down the steep slope to the river that was concealed by birches, willows, ash, and bird cherry. . . . "Wouldn't that be fine," he murmured with a mournful sigh.

"Y-e-s!" continued Chelkash. "I'm thinking how nice it would be for you now to take the train home. . . . Wouldn't you have all the girls running after you! You could choose any one you liked! You could build yourself a new house. . . . I don't think you'll have enough to build a new one though. . . ."

"That's true . . . it won't be enough to build a house. Timber's dear in our parts."

"Well, you could repair the old one. What about a horse? Have you got one?"

"A horse! Yes, I've got a horse, but she's too old, the devil."

"Well, you could buy a horse. Ekh, a f-i-n-e horse! And a cow . . . sheep . . . and poultry. . . . Eh?"

"Oh, don't talk about it! . . . Good Lord! Wouldn't I live then!"

"Y-e-s, brother, it wouldn't be at all bad. . . . I've got some idea of what that kind of life is. I had my own little nest once. . . . My father was one of the richest men in our village. . . ."

Chelkash lazily pulled at the oars. The boat rocked on the waves that were playfully lapping against its sides, barely moving over the dark sea which was becoming more and more boisterous. The two men dreamed as they rocked on the water, thoughtfully gazing around. Wishing to soothe the lad and cheer him up, Chelkash had turned Gavrila's thoughts to his village and had begun the talk in a bantering tone, hiding his smile under his moustache. When questioning Gavrila and reminding him of the joys of peasant life, in which he himself had long been disillusioned, had forgotten and had only recalled now he gradually allowed himself to be carried away by this new train of thought. He stopped questioning the lad about his village and its affairs, and, before he was aware of it, continued in the following strain:

"The main thing in peasant life, brother, is freedom! You're your own master. You have a house. It's not worth much, but it's your own. You have land; only a patch, but it's your own! You are a king on your land! . . . You have a face. . . . You can demand respect from everybody. . . . Isn't that so?" he concluded feelingly.

Gavrila stared at him with curiosity, and he too was carried away by the same feeling. In the course of this conversation he forgot the kind of man he was dealing with and saw before him a peasant, like himself, stuck to the land forever by the sweat of many generations, bound to it by the recollections of childhood, but who had voluntarily run away from it and its cares, and was suffering due punishment for this truancy.

"Yes, brother, what you say is true!" he said. "Oh how true! Look at yourself. What are you now without land? Land is like a mother, you can't forget it so easily."

Chelkash awoke from his musing. . . . He was conscious of that irritating heartburn which he always felt whenever his pride—the pride of the reckless daredevil—was touched by anybody, particularly by one whom he despised.

"Stop sermonizing!" he said fiercely. "Did you think I was talking seriously? . . . You must take me for a fool!"

"You're a funny chap!" Gavrila blurted out, feeling crushed again. "I wasn't talking about you, was I? There's lots of men like you. Lots of them! Ekh! How many unhappy people there are in the world! . . . Roaming around! . . ."

"Here, come and take the oars, you boob!" commanded Chelkash, for some reason restraining the flood of oaths that came rushing up into his throat.

They changed places again, and as he stepped over the bales in the bottom of the boat to reach the stern, Chelkash felt an almost irresistible desire to give Gavrila a push that would send him tumbling into the sea.

The conversation was not resumed, but Chelkash felt the breath of the village even in Gavrila's silence. . . . Musing over the past, he forgot to steer, with the result that the boat, turned by current, drifted out to sea. The waves seemed to understand that the boat had lost its way and began to toss it higher and higher, lightly playing with it, causing kindly blue lights to flash under the oars. And before Chelkash's mental vision floated pictures of the past, of the distant past which was separated from the present by a wall of eleven years of hobo life. He saw himself as a child; he saw his village; his mother, a plump ruddy-cheeked woman with kind grey eyes; he saw his father, a red-bearded giant with a stern face; he saw himself as a bridegroom, and he saw his wife, black-eyed Anfisa, a soft, buxom, cheerful girl with a long plait of hair; he saw himself again as the handsome Guardsman; again he saw his father, now grey and bent by toil, and his mother wrinkled and bowed; he also saw the vision of his return to his village from the army, and how proud his father was of his Grigori, of this handsome, sturdy, bewhiskered soldier. . . . Memory, that scourge of the unhappy, reanimates even the stones of the past, and even pours a drop of honey into the poison that one had once to drink. . . .

Chelkash felt as if he were being fanned by the tender, soothing breath of his native air, which wafted to his ears the kind words of his mother, the grave speech of his earnest peasant father, many forgotten sounds and many fragrant smells of mother earth which has only just thawed, which has only just been ploughed, and is only just being covered with the emerald silken carpet of winter wheat. . . . He felt lonely, uprooted and isolated forever from the way of life which had produced the blood that now flowed in his veins.

"Hey! Where are we going?" suddenly exclaimed Gavrila.

Chelkash started and looked round with the alert gaze of a bird of prey.

"Christ, look where we have drifted to! Lay to the oars! Pull! Pull harder!"

"You've been dreaming, eh," Gavrila asked with a smile.

"I'm tired. . . ."

"So now we won't get caught with these, will we?" Gavrila asked, kicking at the bales at the bottom of the boat.

"No. . . . You can ease your mind on that score. I'll deliver them and get the money. . . . Y-e-s!"

"Five hundred?"

"No less."

"A tidy sum! Wish I had it! Ekh, wouldn't I play a tune with it!"

"On the farm?"

"I should say so! I'd. . . ."

And Gavrila flew off on winged dreams. Chelkash remained silent. His moustache drooped; his right side, splashed by the spray, was dripping wet. His eyes were now sunken and had lost their brightness. Everything rapacious in him had sagged, subdued by humiliating thoughts, which were reflected even from the folds of his grimy blouse.

He swung the boat round abruptly and steered towards something black that loomed out of the water.

The sky was again overcast and rain fell, a fine, warm rain, which pattered merrily as the drops struck the backs of the waves.

"Stop! Be quiet!" commanded Chelkash.

The boat's nose struck the side of a barge.

"Are they asleep, or what, the devils?" growled Chelkash, catching hold with a boat hook of some ropes that were dangling from the deck. "Drop the ladder! Blast it! It must go and rain now! Why couldn't it have rained before! Hey, you swabs! Hey!"

"Is that you, Selkash?" came a voice from above that sounded like the mewing of a cat.

"Come on, drop the ladder!"

"Kalimera, Selkash!"

"Drop the ladder, you hell-smoked devil!" roared Chelkash.

"Oh how angry he eez tonight. . . . Eloy!"

"Up you go, Gavrila!" said Chelkash to his mate.

Within a moment they were on the deck, where three dark-bearded figures were animatedly chattering to each other in a strange lisping tongue and looking over the gunwale down at Chelkash's boat. A fourth, wrapped in a long chlamys, went up to Chelkash, silently shook hands with him, and then glanced suspiciously at Gavrila.

"Get the money by the morning," said Chelkash to him curtly. "I'll turn in now. Come on, Gavrila! Do you want anything to eat?"

"All I want is to sleep . . ." answered Gavrila, and five minutes later he was snoring, while Chelkash, sitting beside him, was trying on somebody's top boot, pensively spitting on the side and whistling a mournful tune through his teeth. Then he stretched out beside Gavrila, put his hands under the back of his head and lay there, twitching his moustache.

The barge rocked gently on the playful water. Something creaked plaintively. The rain pattered softly on the deck. The waves splashed against the side of the barge. . . . And it all sounded so sad, like a cradle song sung by a mother who had no hopes of happiness for her son. . . .

Chelkash bared his teeth, raised his head, looked around, whispered something to himself, and lay down again. . . . He spread out his legs, and this made him look like a huge pair of scissors.

III

He woke up first, looked around anxiously, calmed down at once and looked at Gavrila who was still sleeping, snoring lustily, with a smile spread all over his boyish, healthy, sunburnt face. Chelkash sighed and climbed up a narrow rope ladder. A patch of leaden sky peered down the hatchway. It was already light, but the day was dull and grey, as it usually is in the autumn.

Chelkash returned about two hours later. His face was flushed and his moustaches were dashingly screwed upward. He wore a tunic and buckskin breeches, and a pair of tall, stout top boots. He looked like a huntsman. Although not new, the costume was still sound and suited him well. It made him look broader, concealed his gauntness and gave him a martial appearance.

"Hey, you calf, get up!" he cried, pushing Gavrila with his foot.

Gavrila jumped up. Still half asleep, he failed to recognize Chelkash and stared at him with dull, sleepish eyes. Chelkash burst out laughing.

"You do look fine!" exclaimed Gavrila at last, with a broad smile. "Quite a gentleman!"

"That doesn't take long with us. Well, aren't you a frightened baby! You thought you were going to die a thousand times last night, didn't you?"

"Yes, but judge for yourself. It was the first time I was on a job like that! I might have damned my soul for the rest of my life!"

"Would you come with me again?"

"Again? . . . Well. . . . What can I say? What will I get out of it? Tell me that!"

"Well, suppose you'd get two rainbow ones?"

"Two hundred rubles? That's not so bad. . . . I'd go for that. . . ."

"But wait a minute! What about damning your soul?"

"Well . . . perhaps . . . it won't be damned!" answered Gavrila with a smile. "And if it won't . . . I'll be a made man for life."

Chelkash laughed merrily and said:

"All right! Enough of joking, let's go ashore. . . ."

They were in the boat again, Chelkash at the tiller and Gavrila at the oars. Above them was the grey sky, evenly overcast with clouds. The dull green sea played with the boat, boisterously tossing it on its waves, which were still merrily casting bright salty sprays into the boat. Far ahead loomed a yellow strip of sandy shore, and behind them stretched the vast expanse of the sea, furrowed by packs of waves that were ornamented with fluffy white foam. There, too, in the distance, were numerous ships; far on the left was visible a whole forest of masts, and the white houses of the town, whence came a muffled rumble which, mingling with the splashing of the waves, created fine, powerful music. . . . And over all was cast a thin film of grey mist, which made things seem remote from each other. . . .

"Ekh! There'll be hell let loose this evening!" said Chelkash, nodding in the direction of the sea.

"A storm?" asked Gavrila, ploughing the waves with powerful strokes. He was already drenched from head to foot from the spray which the wind scattered over the sea.

"That's it!" said Chelkash.

Gavrila looked into his face enquiringly. . . .

"Well, how much did they give you?" he asked at last, realizing that Chelkash was not inclined to talk.

"Look!" said Chelkash, showing Gavrila something that he drew from his pocket.

Gavrila saw a roll of coloured bills, and his eyes lit up with joy.

"Ekh! . . . And I thought you were kidding me! How much have you got there?"

"Five hundred and forty!"

"My word!" exclaimed Gavrila in a whisper, following the five hundred and forty rubles with his greedy eyes as Chelkash put the money back into his pocket. "Ekh! If only I had as much as that!"—and he heaved a mournful sigh.

"Won't we have a wonderful time, my lad!" exclaimed Chelkash cheerfully. "Ekh, we'll go on the spree! . . . Don't worry! You'll get your share. . . . I'll give you forty. Does that satisfy you? I'll give it to you right now if you want to?"

"If it's not too much for you. . . . Why not? I'll take it!"

Gavrila trembled with the expectation that gnawed in his breast.

"Oh, you devil's baby! I'll take it, you say! Well, take it, please! Do me a favour! I don't know what to do with all this money! Help me to get rid of it. Take it, do!"

Chelkash held out several bills. Gavrila took them with a trembling hand, dropped the oars and tucked the bills inside his blouse, greedily screwing up his eyes and inhaling noisily, as if he were drinking something very hot. Chelkash watched him with an ironic smile. Gavrila again took up the oars and rowed with downcast eyes nervously, hurriedly, as if afraid of something. His shoulders and ears twitched.

"You're greedy! . . . That's bad. . . . But it's not surprising. . . . You're a peasant . . ." said Chelkash pensively.

"But look what you can do with money!" exclaimed Gavrila, aflush with excitement; and he began to talk rapidly, hurriedly, as if trying to catch up with his thoughts and clutching at words, about life in the village with money and without money, about the honour, abundance and pleasure one can acquire with money.

Chelkash listened attentively, with a grave face and eyes screwed up as if thinking hard. Now and again he smiled with satisfaction.

"Here we are!" he exclaimed, interrupting Gavrila.

A wave lifted the boat and landed it on the sandy beach.

"Well, it's all over now, brother. Pull the boat up higher so that it won't be washed away. They'll come for it. And now we must part! . . . It's eight versts from here to town. I suppose you are going back to town, aren't you?"

A shrewd, good-natured smile lit up Chelkash's face, and his whole bearing indicated that he had thought of something pleasing to himself and surprising for Gavrila. Thrusting his hands in his pocket, he rustled the bills that were lying in them.

"No. . . . I . . . won't go . . . I . . ." gasped Gavrila as if he were choking.

Chelkash looked at him and asked:

"What's ailing you?"

"Nothing . . . only. . . ." Gavrila's face was alternately flushed and ashen-grey, and he stood there wriggling, whether from a desire to hurl himself upon Chelkash, or because he was torn by another desire difficult to fulfill, it was hard to say.

Chelkash felt uneasy at the sight of the lad's agitation and he waited to see what the upshot of it would be.

Gavrila began to laugh in a queer way that sounded more like sobbing. He hung his head, so that Chelkash was unable to see the expression on his face; only his ears were visible, and these grew red and pale by turns.

"Go to the devil!" exclaimed Chelkash, waving his hand in disgust. "Have you fallen in love with me, or what? Stands there wriggling like a girl! Or is it that you don't want to part from me? Now then, you boob! Speak up, or else I'll go away!"

"You'll go away?" shrieked Gavrila.

The sandy, deserted beach shuddered at the sound of this shriek, and the sandy ridges washed up by the waves of the sea seemed to heave. Chelkash too shuddered. Suddenly Gavrila darted towards Chelkash, threw himself at his feet and flinging his arms around his knees gave a sudden tug. Chelkash staggered and dropped heavily to the sand. Grinding his teeth, he raised his long arm and was about to bring his clenched fist down upon Gavrila's head when the blow was checked by the lad's shy and plaintive whisper:

"Be a good fellow! . . . Give me that money! For the sake of Christ, give it to me! It isn't much to you. You got it in one night. . . . Only one night, but it would take me years. . . . Give it to me, and I will pray for you! Always. . . . In three churches. . . . I'll pray for the salvation of your soul! . . . You will only throw the money away. . . . But I, I'd put it in the land! Give me the money! It isn't much to you. You can easily get some more. One night . . . and you are rich! Do me a good turn. After all, you're a lost man. . . . There's nothing before you. . . . But I. . . . Oh. . . . What couldn't I do with the money! Give it to me!"

Chelkash sat on the sand, frightened, amazed and angry, leaning back and propping himself up with his arms, saying not a word, but staring with wide open eyes at the lad who was pressing his head against his knees and whispering, gasping and pleading. At last he pushed the boy away, jumped to his feet, thrust his hand in his pocket, took out several bills and flung them at Gavrila.

"Here you are! Take them . . ." he shouted, trembling with excitement, filled with both intense pity and hatred for this greedy slave. And having thrown the money at him, he felt like a hero.

"I wanted to give you more myself," he said. "My heart was softened last night, thinking of my village. . . . I thought to myself: I'll help the lad. I just waited to see what you would do, whether you would ask for it or not. But you. . . . Ekh! You've got no guts! You're a beggar! . . . Is it worth while tormenting yourself like that for money? Fool! Greedy devils! . . . They've no self respect. . . . They'd sell themselves for five kopecks! . . ."

"Angel! . . . May Christ guard and save you! I'm a different man now. . . . I'm rich!" squealed Gavrila, in a transport of joy, putting the money inside his blouse with a trembling hand. "You are an angel! . . . I shall never forget you, not as long as I live! . . . And I'll tell my wife and my children to pray for you!"

Hearing these rapturous cries and seeing the lad's radiant face distorted by this paroxysm of greed, Chelkash felt that he, a thief, a rake, torn from all his kith and kin, would never become a greedy, low, self-degrading creature like this. No! He would never sink so low! . . . And this thought and feeling, making him conscious of his own freedom, kept him on the deserted seashore with Gavrila.

"You've made me happy for life!" shouted Gavrila again, seizing Chelkash's hand and pressing it against his own face.

Chelkash remained silent, baring his teeth like a wolf. Gavrila kept on chattering:

"And just imagine! As we were coming here I was thinking to myself: I'll give him, meaning you, one c-rr-a-c-k over the head with the oar . . . take the money, and chuck him, meaning you, into the sea. . . . Nobody would miss him, I thought to myself. And even if he was missed, nobody would worry about him. He's not the kind of man anybody would make a fuss about! . . . No use to anybody. Who would stand up for him?!"

Chelkash seized Gavrila by the throat and barked:

"Give that money back!"

Gavrila struggled, but Chelkash's other arm wound round him like a snake. . . . There was a screech of tearing cloth, and Gavrila lay on the sand kicking his legs, his blouse ripped down to the hem, his eyes staring with wild amazement and his fingers clutching the air. Chelkash stood there, tall, straight, thin, with a rapacious look on his face. Baring his teeth he laughed a staccato, sardonic laugh, while his moustache twitched nervously on his sharp angular face. Never in all his life had he been so cruelly insulted, and never had he been so angry.

"Well, are you happy?" he asked Gavrila amidst his laughter. And then, turning his back on him, he strode off in the direction of the town. But he had barely taken half a dozen paces when Gavrila crouched like a cat, jumped to his feet, and with a wide swing of his arm hurled a large pebble at Chelkash, exclaiming fiercely:

"Take that!"

Chelkash gasped, put his hands to his head, staggered, swung round to face Gavrila and fell prone on the sand. Gavrila gazed at the prostrate man dumbfounded. He saw his leg move, he saw him try to raise his head and then stretch out and tremble like a taut string. And then Gavrila dashed off, as fast as his legs could carry him, into the distance, where a shaggy black cloud hung over the misty steppe, and where it was dark. The waves surged up on the sandy beach, merged with it and surged back again. The surf hissed, and the air was filled with spray.

Rain fell at first slowly, but soon in heavy dense streaks, pouring down from the sky. And the streaks wove an entire net of water threads, a net which at once covered the expanses of steppe and sea. Gavrila vanished in this net. For a long time nothing was visible except the rain, and the long body of the man lying on the sand on the seashore. But out of the rain Gavrila reappeared, running as fast as a bird upon the wing. He ran up to Chelkash, dropped to his knees in front of him and turned him over on the sand. His hand came in contact with something warm, red and sticky. . . . He shuddered and started back with horror written on his pallid face.

"Brother, get up!" he whispered into Chelkash's ear amidst the pattering of the rain.

Chelkash came to, pushed Gavrila away and said in a hoarse voice: "Go away! . . ."

"Brother! forgive me! It was the devil who tempted me . . ." whispered Gavrila in a trembling voice, kissing Chelkash's hand.

"Go. . . . Go away . . ." gasped Chelkash.

"Take this sin from my soul! . . . Please! Forgive! . . ."

"For. . . . Go away! . . . Go to hell!" Chelkash suddenly shouted, sitting up. His face was pale and angry, his eyes were dull and heavy, and the lids drooped as if he very much wanted to sleep. "What else do you want? You've done your job. . . . Now go! Clear out!"

And he lunged at grief-stricken Gavrila with his foot, but the effort was too much for him, and he would have sunk back to the sand had not Gavrila put his arm round his shoulders. Chelkash's face was now on a level with Gavrila's. Both were pale and horrible to look at.

"Pht!" and Chelkash spat into his hireling's wide-open eyes.

Gavrila wiped his eyes with his sleeve and whispered:

"Do what you like. . . . I shan't say a word. Forgive me, for the sake of Christ!"

"Worm! . . . You haven't got guts for anything! . . ." shouted Chelkash contemptuously, and then, tearing his blouse from under his coat, he began silently to bandage his head, now and again grinding his teeth with pain. At last he said through his clenched teeth. "Did you take the money?"

"No, I didn't take it, brother! I don't want it! It only causes trouble! . . ."

Chelkash put his hand into the pocket of his coat, drew out the roll of bills, took a rainbow-coloured one from it and put it back in his pocket, and threw the rest at Gavrila, saying:

"Take this and clear out!"

"I won't take it, brother! . . . I can't! Forgive me!"

"Take it, I tell you! . . ." roared Chelkash, rolling his eyes horribly.

"Forgive me . . . and then I'll take it . . ." said Gavrila timidly, dropping down on the rain-drenched sand at Chelkash's feet.

"Liar! You will take it! I know you will, you worm!" said Chelkash in a confident voice. Pulling Gavrila's head up by the hair, he pushed the money into his face and said:

"Take it! Take it! You've earned it! Take it. Don't be afraid! Don't be ashamed of having nearly killed a man! Nobody would punish you for getting rid of a man like me. They would even thank you for it if they got to know of it. Take it!"

Seeing that Chelkash was joking, Gavrila felt relieved. He grasped the money tightly in his hand and enquired in a tearful voice:

"But you do forgive me, brother, don't you, eh?"

"Angel! . . ." answered Chelkash mockingly in the same tone of voice. Rising and swaying on his feet, he said: "Forgive? There's nothing to forgive! You tried to do me in today, and I might try to do you in tomorrow."

"Ekh, brother, brother!" sighed Gavrila, mournfully shaking his head.

Chelkash stood in front of him with a queer smile on his face; and the rag on his head, gradually becoming red, began to look like a Turkish fez.

The rain was now pouring down in torrents. The sea murmured with a hollow sound, and the waves beat furiously and angrily upon the shore.

The two men remained silent.

"Well, good-bye!" said Chelkash ironically, walking off.

He staggered, his legs trembled, and he held his head in a queer way, as if afraid it would drop off.

"Forgive me, brother!" Gavrila begged once again.

"Never mind!" answered Chelkash coldly, continuing on his way.

He staggered on, holding his head with his left hand and slowly twirling his yellow moustache with the right.

Gavrila gazed after him until he vanished in the curtain of rain, which was now pouring from the clouds more densely than ever, in thin, endless streaks, and enveloping the steppe with impenetrable gloom, the colour of steel.

He then took off his soaking cap, crossed himself, looked at the money that he grasped tightly in his hand, heaved a deep sigh of relief, put the money inside his blouse and strode firmly along the beach, in the direction opposite to that in which Chelkash had gone.

The sea howled and hurled large, ponderous waves upon the sandy shore, smashing them into spray and foam. The rain beat heavily upon the water and the land. . . . The wind shrieked. . . . The air all around was filled with whining, roaring, and rumbling. . . . The rain blotted out both sea and sky.

Soon the rain and the spray from the waves washed away the red stain on the spot where Chelkash had lain, and washed out the tracks that Chelkash and the young lad had made on the sandy beach. . . . And nothing was left on the deserted seashore to remind one of the little drama in which these two men had been the actors.

MAKAR CHUDRA

A COLD wet wind blew from the sea, wafting over the steppes the pensive melody of the splashing surf and the rustle of shrubbery on the beach. Now and then its gusts brought shrivelled yellow leaves and whirled them into the flickering flames of the campfire. The gloom of autumnal night around us quivered and receded apprehensively, disclosing for a brief moment the endless steppe on the left, the boundless sea on the right, and opposite me the figure of Makar Chudra, the old Gypsy, who was looking after the horses of his Gypsy camp pitched within fifty paces of where we sat.

Heedless of the cold blasts that blew open his Caucasian coat and mercilessly buffeted his bared hairy chest, he reclined in a graceful vigorous pose with his face towards me, drawing methodically at his huge pipe, emitting thick puffs of smoke through his mouth and nose, staring out over my head into the deathly hushed darkness of the steppes, talking incessantly and making not a single movement to shield himself from the cruel gusts of wind.

"So you're on the tramp? That's fine! You've made a splendid choice, my lad. That's the way: trot around and see things, and when you've seen all you want, lie down and die—that's all!

"Life? Other people?" he went on, having lent a sceptical ear to my protest about his "that's all." "H'm. Why should that worry you? Aren't you Life? Other people live without you and'll live their lives without you. Do you imagine anybody needs you? You're neither bread nor a stick, and nobody wants you.

"To learn and teach, you say? But can you learn how to make people happy? No, you cannot. You get grey hairs first before talking about teaching. Teach what? Every one knows what he wants. Those that are cleverer take what there is to take, the sillier ones get nothing, but every man learns himself.

"They're a curious lot, those people of yours. All herded together and treading on each other's toes when there's so much room in the world," he waved a sweeping hand towards the steppes. "And toiling away all the time. What for? Whom for? Nobody knows. You see a fellow ploughing, and think—there he is sweating out his strength drop by drop on that land, then he'll lie down in it and rot away. He leaves nothing after him, he sees nothing from that field of his and dies as he was born—a fool.

"D'you mean to say he was born to dig the earth and die without having managed to dig a grave for himself? Does he know what freedom is? Has he any idea of the vast and glorious steppe? Does the music of the steppe gladden his heart? He's a slave, from the moment he is born, a slave all his life long, and that's all! What can he do for himself? All he can do is to hang himself, if he learned a little sense.

"Now look at me; at fifty-eight I've seen so much that if you'd write it down on paper it would fill a thousand bags like the one you've got there. You just ask me what places I haven't been to? There aren't such places. You've got no idea of the places I've been to. That's the way to live—gad about the world, and that's all! Don't stay long in one place—it's not worth it! Like day and night that chase each other around the world, you keep chasing yourself away from thoughts of life, so as not to grow sick of it. Once you stop to think you'll get sick of life—that's how it always happens. It happened to me too. Humph! So it did, my lad.

"I was in prison, in Galicia. What am I living on this earth for?—I started to mope, feeling sort of dreary—it's dreary in prison, my lad, ever so dreary! And I felt sick at heart when I looked out of the window at the fields, so sick as though some one were gripping and wrenching my heart. Who can say what he lives for? No one can say it, my lad! And it's no use asking yourself about it. Live, and that's all. Go about and look around, and you'll never be bored. I very nearly hung myself by my belt that time that's a fact!

"Huh! I spoke to a man once. He was a serious man, one of yours, a Russian. You must live, he says, not the way you want, but according to the word of God. Obey the Lord and he will give you everything you ask for. He himself was all in rags and holes. I told him to ask God for a new suit of clothes. He fell into a rage and drove me away, cursing. And he'd just been telling me that one should forgive and love his fellow creatures. He might have forgiven me if what I said offended his lordship. There's a teacher for you! They teach you to eat less, while they themselves eat ten times a day."

He spat into the fire and fell silent, while refilling his pipe. The wind moaned plaintively and softly, the horses whinnied in the darkness, and the tender passionate strains of the *dumka* melody floated up from the Gypsy camp. The beautiful Nonka, Makar's daughter, was singing. I knew that deep throaty-toned voice of hers, that always sounded so strange, discontented and imperious, whether she sang a song or said "good day." The warm pallor of her dark-skinned face was fixed in a look of queenly hauteur, and the deep pools of her dark brown eyes shone with a realization of her own irresistible loveliness and disdain for everything that was not she.

Makar held out his pipe.

"Take a smoke! She sings well, that lass, eh? I should say so! Would you like a girl like that to love you? No? That's right! Never believe girls, and keep away from them. Girls find kissing better and more pleasant than I do smoking a pipe, but once you've kissed her say good-bye to your liberty. She'll bind you to her by invisible strings which you'll never be able to break, and you'll lay your soul at her feet. That's a fact! Beware of the girls! They're all liars! She'll say she loves you more'n anything in the world, but you just prick her with a pin and she'll break your heart. I know a lot about their kind, I do! Well, my lad, d'you want me to tell you a story, a true story? Try to remember it if you can, and it's a free bird you'll be all your life.

"Once upon a time there was a young Gypsy, a young Gypsy named Loiko Zobar. All Hungary and Bohemia and Slavonia and all around the sea everybody knew him—he was a fine lad! There wasn't a village in those parts, but where a half-dozen or so of the inhabitants didn't swear to God they'd kill him. But Loiko went on living, and if he took a fancy to a horse, Zobar'd be curvetting about on that horse even if you was to put a regiment of soldiers to guard it! Ah! He wasn't afraid of anybody, not likely! Why, if the prince of devils with all his pack came to him, he'd as likely as not stick a knife in him, and he'd certainly curse him roundly and send the whole pack off with a flea in its ear—you can take that from me!

"And all the Gypsy camps knew him or had heard of him. All he loved was horses, and nothing more, and even then not for long—he'd ride 'em a bit then sell 'em, and the money was anybody's for the asking. He had nothing that he cherished—if you wanted his heart he'd tear it out of his breast and give it to you, as long as it made you happy. That's the kind he was, my lad!

"Our caravan was wandering at the time through Bukowina—that was about ten years ago. Once, on a night in spring, we were sitting around—myself, the old soldier Danilo who fought under Kossuth, and old Noor and all the others and Radda, Danilo's daughter.

"You know my girl Nonka, don't you? A beautiful maid she is! Well, you couldn't compare her to Radda—too great an honour! There aren't any words to describe that girl Radda. Maybe her beauty could be played on the violin, and even then only by a person who knew that violin as well as he did his own soul.

"She seared the hearts of many a fine lad she did, aye, many a fine lad! In Morava a magnate, an old, shock-headed man saw her and was struck all of a heap. Sat on his horse and stared, shivering as with the ague. He was pranked out like the devil on a holiday, in a rich Ukrainian coat embroidered with gold, and the sword at his side all set in precious stones flashed like lightning whenever his horse stamped its foot, and the blue velvet of his cap was like a bit of sky—he was a big lord, that old gent! He stared and stared, then he says to Radda: 'Hi, give me a kiss, I'll give you my purse!' She just turned away without a word! 'Forgive me if I've offended you, can't you look at me more kindly?' said the old magnate, immediately coming down a peg, and he threw a purse at her feet—a fat purse, brother! And she spurned it in the dust, casual like, with her foot, and that's all.

"'Ah, what a maid!' he groaned, and flicked his horse with his riding crop and was gone in a cloud of dust.

"The next day he came again. 'Who's her father?' he went thundering about the camp. Danilo stepped out. 'Sell me your daughter, take whatever you want!' And Danilo, he says: 'Only the nobility sell everything from their pigs to their conscience, but I fought under Kossuth, and don't traffic in anything!' The other became furious, made a snatch for his sword, but one of the boys stuck a lighted tinder in the horse's ear and he made off with his rider in a flash. We struck tents and moved off. We hadn't been travelling two days when up he dashes again! 'Hi, you,' he says, 'before God and you my conscience is clear, give that maid to me in marriage. I'll share all I have with you, I'm mighty rich!' He was all on fire and swaying in the saddle like feather-grass in the wind. That set us all thinking.

"'Well, daughter, what do you say?' Danilo muttered under his moustache.

"'What would the eagle be if she went into the crow's nest of her own free will?' Radda asked us.

"Danilo laughed, and so did we all.

"'Well said, daughter! Hear that, Sir? Nothing doing! Look among the doves—they're more docile.' And we moved on.

"That gentleman seized his cap, threw it to the ground and galloped away so furiously that the very earth shook. That's the kind of girl Radda was, my lad!

"Yes! Well, one night as we sat around we heard music floating over the steppe. Fine music! It set your blood on fire and lured you into the unknown. That music, we all felt, made one yearn for something after which, if you got it, life would no longer be worth living, unless it was, as kings over all the earth, my lad!

"Well, a horse loomed out of the darkness, and on the horse a man sat and played as he approached us. He drew up at the campfire, ceased playing and smiled down at us.

"'Ah, why, that's you, Zobar!' Danilo cried out to him joyfully. Yes, that was Loiko Zobar!

"His moustaches lay on his shoulders and mingled with his locks, his eyes were as bright as stars and his smile was like the sun so help me God! He and his horse might have been forged of a single piece of iron. There he stood red as blood in the firelight, his teeth flashing in a smile! Damned if I didn't love him then more than I loved myself, even before he had spoken a word to me or had as much as noticed my existence!

"Yes, my lad, that's the kind of man he was! He'd look into your eyes and captivate your soul, and you wouldn't be the least bit ashamed of it, only feel proud about it. With a man like that you feel nobler yourself. Such men are rare, my friend! Perhaps that's better so. If there'd be too much of a good thing in this world it wouldn't be looked on as a good thing. Aye! Well, let's get on with the story.

"Radda she says: 'You play well, Loiko! Who made you such a sweet-toned delicate fiddle?' He laughed—'I made it myself! And I made it not of wood, but from the breast of a young girl whom I loved dearly, and the strings I play on are her heartstrings. The fiddle plays a little false, but I know how to handle the bow!'

"Our breed, you know, tries straight away to befog a girl's eyes, so they be dimmed with sad yearning for a fellow without kindling his own heart. That was Loiko's way too. But Radda was not to be caught that way. She turned away with a yawn and said: 'And people said Zobar was clever and adroit—what liars!' With that she walked away.

"'Oho, pretty maid, you've got sharp teeth!' said Loiko with a flashing eye, getting off his horse. 'How do you do, brothers! Well, here I am come to you!'

"'Welcome, guest!' said Danilo in reply. We kissed, had a talk and went to bed. . . . We slept soundly. In the morning we saw that Zobar's head was tied up with a rag. What's that? Oh, his horse accidentally hurt him with its hoof while he was asleep.

"Ha-a! We guessed who that horse was and smiled into our moustaches, and Danilo smiled too. Well, wasn't Loiko worthy of Radda? I should think so! However fair a maid may be, she has a narrow, petty soul, and though you'd hang a pood of gold round her neck she'd never be any better than she was. Well, anyway!

"We lived a pretty long time on that spot, things were going well with us and Zobar was with us. That was a comrade for you! Wise like an old man, informed on everything and knew how to read and write Russian and Magyar. When he'd start speaking you'd forget about sleep and could listen to him for ages! As for playing—well salt my hide if there's another man in the world could play like that! He'd draw his bow across the strings and your heart'd begin to flutter, then he'd draw it again and it'd stop beating while you listened, and he just played and smiled. You felt like crying and laughing one and the same time when listening to him. Now you'd hear some one moaning bitterly, pleading for help and lacerating your heart as with a knife; now the steppe telling the heavens a fairy tale, a sad tale; now a maid weeping, bidding farewell to her beloved! And now a valiant youth calling his beloved to the steppe. Then suddenly—heigh-ho! A brave merry tune fills the air, and the very sun, it seems, bids fair to start a jig up in the sky! Yes, my lad, that's how it was!

"Every fibre in your body understood that song, and you became its slave, body and soul. If Loiko had then cried out: 'To knives, comrades!' we'd have snatched up our knives as one man and followed him blindly. He could do anything he wanted with a man, and everybody loved him, loved him mightily—only Radda had no eyes for the lad. That wouldn't have been so bad, worse was she mocked him. She smote that lad's heart sorely, aye sorely! He'd gnash his teeth, Loiko would, pulling at his moustache. Eyes darker than an abyss, and sometimes with a gleam of something fit to harrow up the soul. At night he'd go far out into the steppe, would Loiko, and his fiddle would weep till morning, weep over the death of Loiko's liberty. And we lay listening and thinking: what's to be done? We knew that if two stones are rolling down on each other it's no use getting between them—they'd crush you. That's how things were.

"Well, we all sat assembled, discussing affairs. Then things got dull. So Danilo asks Loiko: 'Sing a song, Loiko, something to cheer the soul!' The lad glanced at Radda who was lying at a little distance with her face looking up into the sky, and drew his bow across the strings. The fiddle spoke as though it were really a maiden's heart, and Loiko sang:

> *Hey-ho! A flame the heart doth feed,*
> *Vast the steppe and wide!*
> *Fleet as the wind my gallant steed,*
> *Strong-armed rider astride!*

"Radda turned her head, and rising on her elbow, smiled mockingly into the singer's eyes. He reddened like the dawn.

Hey-ho-hey! Up comrade arise!
Onward let us race!
Where steppe in deepest darkness lies,
To waiting dawn's embrace!
Hey-ho! We fly to meet the day,
Soaring above the plain!
Touch not thee in passing, pray
The beauteous moon with thy mane!

"Did he sing! Nobody sings like that any more! And Radda says, letting the words drop:

"'You shouldn't fly so high, Loiko. You might fall and come down on your nose in a puddle and wet your moustache, be careful.' Loiko glared fiercely at her and said nothing—he swallowed it and went on singing:

Hey-ho-hey! Lest daybreak's flush
Overtake us in idle slumber,
Away, away, ere for shame we blush,
And men begin to wonder!

"'What a song!' said Danilo, 'never heard anything like it before, may the Devil make a pipe out of me if I lie!' Old Noor twitched his moustache and shrugged his shoulders and everybody was delighted with that brave song of Zobar's! Only Radda didn't like it.

"'That's how a wasp once buzzed when he tried to imitate the cry of an eagle,' said she, and it was as if she had thrown snow over us.

"'Maybe you'd like a taste of the whip, Radda?' Danilo said, starting up, but Zobar threw his cap on the ground and spoke, his face as dark as the earth:

"'Stop, Danilo! A spirited horse needs a steel bridle! Give your daughter to me as wife!'

"'Now you've said something!' said Danilo with a smile. 'Take her if you can!'

"'Good!' said Loiko and spoke thus to Radda:

"'Well, lass, listen to me a while and don't put on airs! I've seen a lot of your sisterhood in my time, aye quite a lot! But not one of them ever touched my heart like you have. Ah, Radda, you have snared my soul! Well? What's to be must needs be, and . . . the steed does not exist on which one could escape from one's self! . . . I take you to wife before God, my conscience, your father and all these people. But mind, you are not to oppose my will—I am a free man and will live the way I want!' And he went up to her, his teeth clenched and eyes flashing. We saw him holding out his hand to her—now, thought we, Radda has bridled the horse of the steppe! Suddenly we saw his hand go up and he fell, hitting the ground with the back of his head with a crash! . . .

"Good heavens! It was as if a bullet had struck the lad in the heart. Radda, it appears, had swept the whiplash round his legs and pulled it, sending him off his feet.

"There she was lying back again without stirring, with a mocking smile on her face. We waited to see what would happen next. Loiko sat on the ground clutching his head as though afraid it would burst. Then he got up quietly and walked off into the steppe without a glance at anyone. Noor whispered to me: 'Keep your eye on him!' And I crawled after Zobar into the darkness of the steppe. Yes, my lad!"

Makar knocked the ashes out of his pipe and began refilling it again. I drew my coat closer about me and lay looking at his old face, blackened by the sun and winds. He was whispering to himself, shaking his head sternly; his grizzled moustache moved up and down and the wind stirred the hair on his head. He was like an old oak tree seared by lightning, but still strong and sturdy and proud of its strength. The sea still carried on a whispered converse with the shore and the wind still carried its whispers over the steppe. Nonka had stopped singing, and the clouds that had gathered in the sky made the autumn night still darker.

"Loiko dragged his feet wearily along, his head bent and hands hanging nervelessly by his sides, and when he reached a ravine by the stream he sat down on a boulder and groaned. It was a groan that made my heart bleed for pity, but I didn't go up to him. Grief won't be comforted by words, will it? That's just it! He sat on for an hour, then another, and a third, just sat without stirring.

"And I was lying on the ground nearby. It was a bright night, the whole steppe was bathed in silver moonlight and you could see far away in the distance.

"Suddenly, I saw Radda hurrying towards us from the camp.

"That cheered me up! 'Ah, splendid!' I thought, 'brave lass, Radda!' She drew close, but he hadn't heard her coming. She put her hand on his shoulder; Loiko started, unclasped his hands and raised his head. Then he leapt to his feet and gripped his knife! 'Ah, he'll knife the maid, I thought,' and I was just going to shout out to the camp and run to them when I suddenly heard:

"'Drop it! I'll smash your head!' I looked—there was Radda with a pistol in her hand aimed at Zobar's head. There's a hell-cat for you! Well, I thought, they're now matched in strength, I wonder what'll happen next?

"'Look here!'—Radda thrust the pistol into her waistband—'I didn't come here to kill you, but to make up—drop the knife!' He dropped it and looked sullenly into her eyes! It was a sight, brother! There were two people glaring at each other like animals at bay, and both such fine, brave people. There were just the shining moon and I looking on, that's all.

"'Now, listen to me, Loiko. I love you!' said Radda. He merely shrugged, as though tied hand and foot.

"'I've seen brave youths, but you're braver and better in face and soul. Any of them would have shaven their moustache had I so much as winked my eye, all of them would have fallen at my feet had I wished it. But what's the sense? They're none too brave anyway, and I'd have made them all womanish. There are few brave Gypsies left in the world as it is, very few, Loiko. I never loved anybody, Loiko, but you I love. But I love liberty too! I love liberty, Loiko, more than I do you. But I cannot live without you, as you cannot live without me. So I want you to be mine, body and soul, do you hear?' He smiled a twisted smile.

"'I hear! It cheers the heart to hear your speeches! Say some more!'

"'This more I want to say, Loiko: no matter how you twist I'll have my way with you, you'll be mine. So don't waste time—my kisses and caresses are awaiting you, and I shall kiss you sweetly, Loiko! Under my kisses you shall forget your adventurous life . . . and your lively songs which so gladden the hearts of the Gypsy lads will be heard no more in the steppe—you shall sing other songs, tender love songs to me, Radda. . . . Waste not time then—I have spoken, therefore tomorrow you shall obey me like the youth who obeys his elder comrade. You shall bow the knee to me before the whole Gypsy camp and kiss my right hand—then I shall be your wife.'

"So that's what she was after, the mad girl! It was unheard of! It had been the custom once among the Montenegrins, so the old men said, but never among the Gypsies! Well, my lad, can you think of anything funnier than that? Not if you racked your brains a year, you wouldn't!

"Loiko recoiled and his cry rang out over the steppe like that of a man wounded in the breast. Radda winced but did not betray herself.

"'Well, good-bye till tomorrow, and tomorrow you will do as I bade you. Do you hear, Loiko?'

"'I hear! I will,' groaned Zobar and held his arms out to her. She went without even turning her head, and he swayed like a tree broken by the wind and dropped to the ground, sobbing and laughing.

"That is what the accursed Radda did to the poor lad. I had a job bringing him to his senses.

"Ah well! Why the devil should people have to drain the cup of misery? Who cares to hear a human heart moaning in pain and grief? Make it out if you can! . . .

"I went back to the camp and told the old men all about it. They thought the matter over and decided to wait and see what would happen. And this is what happened. When we all gathered next evening around the campfire Loiko joined us. He was gloomy and had become terribly haggard overnight and his eyes were sunken. He cast them down and, without raising them, said to us:

"'I want to tell you something, comrades. I looked into my heart this night and found no place therein for the old carefree life of mine. Radda alone dwells in it—and that's all! There she is, beautiful Radda, smiling like a queen! She loves her liberty more than me, and I love her more than my liberty, and I have decided to bend my knee to her, as she bade me, so that all may see how her beauty has conquered brave Loiko Zobar, who until he knew her used to play with the girls like a gerfalcon with the ducks. After that she will become my wife and will kiss and caress me, so that I will have no more desire to sing you songs and will not regret my liberty! Is that right, Radda?' He raised his eyes and looked darkly at her. She silently and sternly nodded her head and pointed her hand to her feet. And we looked on, understanding nothing. We even felt like going away, not to see Loiko Zobar prostrate himself at a maid's feet, even though that maid were Radda. We felt sort of ashamed, and sorry and sad.

"'Well!' cried Radda to Zobar.

"'Aha, don't be in a hurry, there's plenty of time, you'll have more than enough of it . . .' he retorted with a laugh. And that laugh had a ring of steel in it.

"'So that's all I wanted to tell you, comrades! What next? It remains next but to test whether Radda has so strong a heart as she showed me. I'll test it—forgive me, brothers!'

"Before we could fathom these words Radda lay stretched on the earth with Zobar's curved knife sunk to the hilt in her breast. We were horror-struck.

"And Radda pulled out the knife, threw it aside, and pressing a lock of her black hair to the wound, said loudly and audibly with a smile:

"'Farewell, Loiko! I knew you would do that! . . .' and she died. . . .

"D'you grasp the kind of maid that was, my lad? A hell of a maid she was, may I be damned to eternity!

"'Oh! Now I'll kneel at your feet, proud queen!' Loiko's loud cry echoed all over the steppe, and throwing himself to the ground he pressed his lips to the feet of dead Radda and lay motionless. We took off our caps and stood in silence.

"What do you say to that, my lad? Aye, that's just it! Noor said: 'We ought to bind him! . . .' No hand would lift to bind Loiko Zobar, not a hand would lift, and Noor knew it. He waved his hand and turned away. And Danilo picked up the knife which Radda had cast aside and gazed long at it, his moustache twitching. The blade of that knife, so curved and sharp, was still wet with Radda's blood. And then Danilo went up to Zobar and stuck the knife into his back over the heart. For he was Radda's father, was Danilo the old soldier!

"'There you are!' said Loiko in a clear voice, turning to Danilo, and he followed on the heels of Radda.

"And we stood looking. There lay Radda, pressing a lock of hair to her bosom, and her open eyes stared into the blue sky while at her feet brave Loiko Zobar lay stretched. His face was covered by his locks and you couldn't see his face.

"We stood lost in thought. Old Danilo's moustaches trembled and his bushy brows were knitted. He stared at the sky and said nothing, while Noor, grey old Noor, lay down with his face on the ground and all his old body was racked with sobs.

"There was something to cry over, my lad!

". . . So you're going on the tramp—well, go your way, don't turn off the road. You go straight on. Maybe you won't go to the dogs. That's all, my lad!"

Makar fell silent, and putting the pipe into his pouch, wrapped his coat over his chest. Rain began to fall in a drizzle, the wind was rising, the sea growled and rumbled angrily. The horses one by one came up to the dying campfire and regarding us with their big intelligent eyes stopped motionless around us in a dense ring.

"Hey, hey, ho!" Makar cried to them kindly, and patting the neck of his favourite black horse, said, turning to me:

"Time to go to sleep!" and, drawing his coat over his head and stretching his great length out on the ground he fell silent. I did not feel like sleeping. I gazed into the darkness of the steppe and before my eyes swum the queenly beautiful image of proud Radda. She was pressing a lock of hair to the wound in her breast and through her delicate swarthy fingers the blood oozed drop by drop, falling to the ground like flaming-red little stars.

Following close on her heels there floated the vision of the brave Gypsy lad Loiko Zobar. His face was screened by thick black locks from under which big cold tears fell fast. . . .

The rain grew heavier and the sea was chanting a mournful solemn dirge to the proud pair of Gypsy lovers—to Loiko Zobar and to Radda, the daughter of the old soldier Danilo.

And they both hovered silently in the misty darkness, and the dashing Loiko, try as he may, was unable to catch up with the proud Radda.

TWENTY-SIX MEN AND A GIRL

WE WERE twenty-six men, twenty-six living machines cooped up in a dark hole of a basement where from morn till night we kneaded dough, making pretzels and cracknels. The windows of our basement faced a sunken area lined with bricks that were green with slime; the windows outside were encased in a close-set iron grating, and no ray of sunshine could reach us through the panes which were covered with meal. Our boss had fenced the windows off to prevent any of his bread going to beggars or to those of our comrades who were out of work and starving—our boss called us a bunch of rogues and gave us tainted tripe for dinner instead of meat. . . .

Stuffy and crowded was life in that stony dungeon beneath a low-hanging ceiling covered by soot and cobwebs. Life was hard and sickening within those thick walls smeared with dirt stains and mildew. . . . We got up at five in the morning, heavy with lack of sleep, and at six, dull and listless, we sat down to the table to make pretzels and cracknels out of the dough our comrades had prepared while we were sleeping. And all day long, from morning till ten o'clock at night some of us sat at the table kneading the stiff dough and swaying the body to fight numbness, while others were mixing flour and water. And all day long the simmering water in the cauldron where the pretzels were cooking gurgled pensively and sadly, and the baker's shovel clattered angrily and swiftly on the hearthstone, throwing slippery cooked pieces of dough onto the hot bricks. From morning till night the wood burned at one end of the oven, and the ruddy glow of the flames flickered on the bakery walls, as though grinning at us. The huge oven resembled the ugly head of some fantastic monster thrust up from under the floor, its wide-open jaws ablaze with glowing fire breathing incandescent flames and heat at us, and watching our ceaseless toil through two sunken air-holes over its forehead. These two hollows were like eyes— the pitiless impassive eyes of a monster; they looked at us with an invariable dark scowl, as though weary with looking at slaves of whom

42

nothing human could be expected, and whom they despised with the cold contempt of wisdom.

Day in, day out, amid the meal dust and the grime that we brought in on our feet from the yard, in the smelly stuffiness of the hot basement, we kneaded the dough and made pretzels which were sprinkled with our sweat, and we hated our work with a fierce hatred, and never ate what our hands had made, preferring black rye bread to pretzels. Sitting at a long table facing one another—nine men on each side— our hands and fingers worked mechanically through the long hours, and we had grown so accustomed to our work that we no longer watched our movements. And we had grown so accustomed to one another that each of us knew every furrow on his comrades' faces. We had nothing to talk about, we were used to that, and were silent all the time—unless we swore, for there is always something one can swear at a man for, especially one's comrade. But we rarely swore at each other—is a man to blame if he is half-dead, if he is like a stone image, if all his senses are blunted by the crushing burden of toil? Silence is awful and painful only for those who have said all there is to say; but to people whose words are still unspoken, silence is simple and easy. . . . Sometimes we sang, and this is how our song would begin: during the work somebody would suddenly heave a deep sigh, like a weary horse, and begin softly to sing one of those long-drawn songs whose mournfully tender melody always lighten the heavy burden of the singer's heart. One of the men would sing while we listened in silence to the lonely song, and it would fade and die away beneath the oppressive basement ceiling like the languishing flames of a campfire in the steppe on a wet autumn night, when the grey sky hangs over the earth like a roof of lead. Then another singer would join the first, and two voices would float drearily and softly in the stuffy heat of our crowded pen. And then suddenly several voices at once would take up the song—it would be lashed up like a wave, grow stronger and louder, and seem to break open the damp, heavy walls of our stony prison. . . .

All the twenty-six are singing; loud voices, brought to harmony by long practice, fill the workshop; the song is cramped for room; it breaks against the stone walls, moaning and weeping, and stirs the heart with a gentle prickly pain, reopening old wounds and wakening anguish in the soul. . . . The singers draw deep and heavy sighs; one will suddenly break off and sit listening for a long time to his comrades singing, then his voice will mingle again in the general chorus. Another will cry out dismally: "Ach!" singing with closed eyes, and maybe he sees the broad torrent of sound as a road leading far away, a wide road lit up by the brilliant sun, and he himself walking along it. . . .

The flames in the oven still flicker, the baker's shovel still scrapes on the brick, the water in the cauldron still bubbles and gurgles, the fire-light on the wall still flutters in silent laughter. . . . And we chant out, through words not our own, the dull ache within us, the gnawing grief of living men deprived of the sun, the grief of slaves. And so we lived, twenty-six men, in the basement of a big stone house, and so hard was our life, that it seemed as though the three stories of the house were built on our shoulders. . . .

Besides our songs there was something else that we loved and cher-ished, something that perhaps filled the place of the sun for us. On the second floor of our house there was a gold embroidery workshop, and there, among many girl hands, lived sixteen-year-old Tanya, a house-maid. Every morning a little pink face with blue merry eyes would be pressed to the pane of the little window cut into the door of our work-shop leading into the passage, and a sweet ringing voice would call out to us:

"Jail-birdies! Give me some pretzels!"

We would all turn our heads to the sound of that clear voice and look kindly and joyfully at the pure girlish face that smiled at us so sweetly. We liked to see the nose squashed against the glass, the little white teeth glistening from under rosy lips parted in a smile. We would rush to open the door for her, jostling each other, and there she would be, so winsome and sunny, holding out her apron, standing before us with her little head slightly tilted, and her face all wreathed in smiles. A thick long braid of chestnut hair hung over her shoulder on her breast. We grimy, ignorant, ugly men look up at her—the threshold rises four steps above the floor—look up at her with raised heads and wish her good morning, and our words of greeting are special words, found only for her. When we speak to her our voices are softer, our joking lighter. Everything we have for her is special. The baker draws out of the oven a shovelful of the crustiest browned pretzels and shoots them adroitly into Tanya's apron.

"Mind the boss doesn't catch you!" we warn her. She laughs rogu-ishly and cries merrily:

"Good-bye jail-birdies!" and vanishes in a twinkling like a little mouse.

And that is all. . . . But long after she was gone we talk about her— we say the same things we said the day before and earlier, because she, and we, and everything around us are the same they were the day be-fore and earlier. . . . It is very painful and hard when a man lives, and nothing around him changes, and if it doesn't kill the soul in him, the longer he lives the more painful does the immobility of things sur-rounding him become. . . . We always talked of women in a way that

sometimes made us feel disgusted with ourselves and our coarse shameless talk. That is not surprising, since the women we knew did not probably deserve to be talked of in any other way. But of Tanya we never
said a bad word; no one of us ever dared to touch her with his hand and
she never heard a loose joke from any of us. Perhaps it was because she
never stayed long—she would flash before our gaze like a star falling
from the heavens and vanish. Or perhaps it was because she was small
and so very beautiful, and everything that is beautiful inspires respect,
even with rough men. Moreover, though hard labour was turning us
into dumb oxen, we were only human beings, and like all human beings, could not live without an object of worship. Finer than she there
was nobody about us, and nobody else paid attention to us men living
in the basement—though there were dozens of tenants in the house.
And finally—probably chiefly—we regarded her as something that belonged to us, something that existed thanks only to our pretzels; we
made it our duty to give her hot pretzels, and this became our daily sac-
rifice to the idol, almost a holy rite, that endeared her to us ever more
from day to day. Besides pretzels we gave Tanya a good deal of advice—
to dress warmly, not to run quickly upstairs, not to carry heavy bundles
of firewood. She listened to our counsels with a smile, retorted with a
laugh and never obeyed them, but we did not take offence—we were
satisfied to show our solicitude for her.

Often she asked us to do things for her. She would, for instance, ask
us to open a refractory door in the cellar or chop some wood, and we
would gladly and with a peculiar pride do these things for her and anything else she asked.

But when one of us asked her to mend his only shirt, she sniffed
scornfully and said:

"Catch me! Not likely!"

We enjoyed a good laugh at the silly fellow's expense, and never
again asked her to do anything. We loved her—and there all is said. A
man always wants to foist his love on somebody or other, though it frequently oppresses, sometimes sullies, and his love may poison the life
of a fellow creature, for in loving he does not respect the object of his
love. We had to love Tanya, for there was no one else we could love.

At times one of us would suddenly begin to argue something like
this:

"What's the idea of making such a fuss over the kid? What's there so
remarkable about her anyway?"

We'd soon brusquely silence the fellow who spoke like that—we had
to have something we could love: we found it, and loved it, and what
we twenty-six loved stood for each of us, it was our holy of holies, and
anybody who went against us in this matter was our enemy. We love,

perhaps, what is not really good, but then there are twenty-six of us, and we therefore want the object of our adoration to be held sacred by others.

Our love is no less onerous than hate . . . and, perhaps, that is why some stiff-necked people claim that our hate is more flattering than love. . . . But why do they not shun us if that is so?

In addition to the pretzel bakehouse our boss had a bun bakery. It was situated in the same house, and only a wall divided it from our hole. The bun bakers, however, of whom there were four, held themselves aloof from us, considered their work cleaner than ours, and themselves, therefore, better men; they never visited our workshop, and treated us with mocking scorn whenever they met us in the yard. Neither did we visit them—the boss banned such visits for fear we would steal buns. We did not like the bun bakers, because we envied them—their work was easier than ours, they got better wages, they were fed better, they had a roomy, airy workshop, and they were all so clean and healthy, and hence so odious. We, on the other hand, were all a yellow grey-faced lot; three of us were ill with syphilis, some were scabby, and one was crippled by rheumatism. On holidays and off-days they used to dress up in suits and creaking high boots, two of them possessed accordions, and all used to go out for a stroll in the park, whilst we were dressed in filthy tatters, with rags or bast shoes on our feet, and the police wouldn't let us into the park—now, could we love the bun bakers?

And one day we learned that their chief baker had taken to drink, that the boss had dismissed him and taken on another in his place, and that the new man was an ex-soldier who went about in a satin waistcoat and had a watch on a gold chain. We were curious to have a look at that dandy, and every now and then one of us would run out into the yard in the hope of seeing him.

But he came to our workshop himself. Kicking open the door he stood in the doorway, smiling, and said to us:

"Hullo! How do you do, boys!"

The frosty air rushing through the door in a smoky cloud eddied round his feet, while he stood in the doorway looking down at us, his large yellow teeth flashing from under his fair swaggering moustache. His waistcoat was indeed unique—a blue affair, embroidered with flowers, and all glittering, with buttons made of some kind of red stone. The chain was there too. . . .

He was a handsome fellow, was that soldier—tall, strong, with ruddy cheeks and big light eyes that had a nice look in them—a kind, clean look. On his head he wore a white stiffly starched cap, and from under an immaculately clean apron peeped the pointed toes of a highly polished pair of fashionable boots.

Our chief baker politely asked him to close the door. He complied unhurriedly and began questioning us about the boss. We fell over each other telling him that the boss was a skinflint, a crook, a scoundrel and a tormentor—we told him everything there was to tell about the boss that couldn't be put in writing here. The soldier listened, twitching his moustache and regarding us with that gentle, clear look of his.

"You've a lot of girls around here . . ." he said suddenly.

Some of us laughed politely, others pulled sugary faces, and some one informed the soldier that there were nine bits in the place.

"Use 'em?" asked the soldier with a knowing wink.

Again we laughed, a rather subdued, embarrassed laugh. . . . Many of us would have liked to make the soldier believe they were as gay lads as he was, but they couldn't do it, none of us could do it. Somebody confessed as much, saying quietly:

"How comes we. . . ."

"M'yes, you're a long way off!" said the soldier convincedly, subjecting us to a close scrutiny. "You're not . . . er, up to the mark. . . . Ain't got the character . . . the proper shape . . . you know, looks! Looks is what a woman likes about a man! Give her a regular body . . . everything just so! Then of course she likes a bit of muscle. . . . Likes an arm to be an arm, here's the stuff!"

The soldier pulled his right hand out of his pocket, with the sleeve rolled back to the elbow, and held it up for us to see. . . . He had a strong, white arm covered with shining golden hair.

"The leg, the chest—everything must be firm. . . . And then a man's got to be properly dressed . . . in shipshape form. . . . Now, the women just fall for me. Mind you, I don't call 'em or tempt 'em—they hang about my neck five at a time. . . ."

He sat down on a sack of flour and spent a long time in telling us how the women loved him and how dashingly he treated them. Then he took his leave, and when the door closed behind him with a squeak, we sat on in a long silence, meditating over him and his stories. Then suddenly everybody spoke up at once, and it transpired that we had all taken a liking to him. Such a simple, nice fellow, the way he came in, sat down, and chatted. Nobody ever came to see us, nobody talked to us like that, in a friendly way. . . . And we kept on talking about him and his future success with the seamstresses, who, on meeting us in the yard, either steered clear of us with lips offensively pursed, or bore straight down on us as though we did not stand in their path at all. And we only admired them, in the yard or when they passed our windows, dressed in cute little caps and fur coats in the winter, and in flowery hats with bright coloured parasols in the summer. But among ourselves we spoke of these girls in a way that, had they heard us, would have made them mad with shame and insult.

"I hope he doesn't . . . spoil little Tanya!" said the chief baker suddenly in a tone of anxiety.

We were all struck dumb by this statement. We had somehow forgotten Tanya—the soldier seemed to have blotted her out with his large, handsome figure. Then a noisy argument broke out: some said that Tanya would not stand for it, some asserted that she would be unable to resist the soldier's charms, and others proposed to break the fellow's bones in the event of him making love to Tanya. Finally, all decided to keep a watch on the soldier and Tanya, and warn the kid to beware of him. . . . That put a stop to the argument.

About a month passed. The soldier baked buns, went out with the seamstresses, frequently dropped in to see us, but never said anything about his victories—all he did was to turn up his moustache and lick his chops.

Tanya came every morning for her pretzels and was invariably gay, sweet and gentle. We tried to broach the subject of the soldier with her—she called him "a pop-eyed dummy" and other funny names and that set our minds at rest. We were proud of our little girl when we saw how the seamstresses clung to the soldier. Tanya's attitude towards him bucked us all up, and under her influence as it were, we ourselves began to evince towards him an attitude of scorn. We loved her more than ever, and greeted her more gladly and kindly in the mornings.

One day, however, the soldier dropped in on us a little the worse for drink, sat down and began to laugh, and when we asked him what he was laughing at, he explained:

"Two of them have had a fight over me. . . . Lida and Grusha. . . . You should have seen what they did to each other! A regular scream, ha-ha! One of 'em grabbed the other by the hair, dragged her all over the floor into the passage, then got on top of her . . . ha-ha-ha! Scratched each other's mugs, tore their clothes. . . . Wasn't that funny! Now, why can't these females have a straight fight? Why do they scratch, eh?"

He sat on a bench, looking so clean and healthy and cheerful, laughing without a stop. We said nothing. Somehow he was odious to us this time.

"Why am I such a lucky devil with the girls? It's a scream! Why, I just wink my eye and the trick's done!"

He raised his white hands covered with glossy hairs and brought them down on his knees with a slap. He surveyed us with a look of pleased surprise, as though himself genuinely astonished at the lucky turn of his affairs with the ladies. His plump ruddy physiognomy shone with smug pleasure and he repeatedly passed his tongue over his lips.

Our chief baker angrily rattled his shovel on the hearth and suddenly said sarcastically:

"It's no great fun felling little fir trees—I'd like to see what you'd do with a pine!"

"Eh, what? Were you talking to me?" asked the soldier.

"Yes, you. . . ."

"What did you say?"

"Never mind. . . . Let it lay. . . ."

"Here, hold on! What's it all about? What d'you mean—pine?"

Our baker did not reply. His shovel moved swiftly in the oven, tossing in boiled pretzels and discharging the baked ones noisily onto the floor where boys sat threading them on bast strings. He seemed to have forgotten the soldier. But the latter suddenly got excited. He rose to his feet and stepped up to the oven, exposing himself to the imminent danger of being struck in the chest by the shovel handle that whisked spasmodically in the air.

"Now, look the—who d'you mean? That's an insult. . . . Why, there ain't a girl that could resist me! No fear! And here are you, hinting things against me. . . ."

Indeed, he appeared to be genuinely offended. Evidently the only source of his self-respect was his ability to seduce women: perhaps this ability was the only living attribute he could boast, the only thing that made him feel a human being.

There are some people for whom life holds nothing better or higher than a malady of the soul or flesh. They cherish it throughout life, and it is the sole spring of life to them. While suffering from it they nourish themselves on it. They complain about it to people and in this manner command the interest of their neighbours. They exact a toll of sympathy from people, and this is the only thing in life they have. Deprive them of that malady, cure them of it, and they will be utterly miserable, because they will lose the sole sustenance of their life and become empty husks. Sometimes a man's life is so poor that he is perforce obliged to cultivate a vice and thrive on it. One might say that people are often addicted to vice through sheer boredom.

The soldier was stung to the quick. He bore down on our baker, whining:

"No, you tell me—who is it?"

"Shall I tell you?" said the baker, turning on him suddenly.

"Well?"

"D'you know Tanya?"

"Well?"

"Well, there you are! See what you can do there. . . ."

"Me?"

"Yes, you."

"Her? Easier'n spitting!"

"We'll see!"

"You'll see! Ha-a!"

"Why, she'll. . . ."

"It won't take a month!"

"You're cocky, soldier, ain't you?"

"A fortnight! I'll show you! Who did you say? Tanya? Pshaw!"

"Come on, get out, you're in the way!"

"A fortnight, and the trick's done! Oh, you! . . ."

"Get out!"

The baker suddenly flew into a rage and brandished his shovel. The soldier fell back in amazement, then regarded us all for a while in silence, muttered grimly "All right!" and went out.

All through this argument we had kept our peace, our interest having been engaged in the conversation. But when the soldier left we all broke out into loud and animated speech.

Somebody cried out to the baker:

"That's a bad business you've started, Pavel!"

"Get on with your work!" snapped the baker.

We realized that the soldier had been put on his high ropes and that Tanya was in danger. Yet, while realizing this, we were all gripped by a tense but thrilling curiosity as to what would be the outcome of it. Would Tanya hold her own against the soldier? We almost unanimously voiced the conviction:

"Tanya? She'll hold her ground! She ain't easy prey!"

We were terribly keen on testing our idol; we assiduously tried to convince each other that our idol was a staunch idol and would come out on top in this engagement. We ended up by expressing our doubts as to whether we had sufficiently goaded the soldier, fearing that he would forget the wager and that we would have to prick his conceit some more. Henceforth a new exciting interest had come into our lives, something we had never known before. We argued among ourselves for days on end; we all somehow seemed to have grown cleverer, spoke better and more. It seemed as though we were playing a sort of game with the devil, and the stake on our side was Tanya. And when we had learned from the bun bakers that the soldier had started to "make a dead set for Tanya" our excitement rose to such a furious pitch and life became such a thrilling experience for us that we did not even notice how the boss had taken advantage of our wrought up feelings to throw in extra work by raising the daily knead to fourteen poods of dough. We didn't even seem to tire of the work. Tanya's name was all day long on our lips. And we awaited her morning visits with a peculiar impatience. At times we fancied that when she came in to see us it would be a different Tanya, not the one we always knew.

We told her nothing, however, about the wager. We never asked her any questions and treated her in the same good-natured loving way. But something new had crept into our attitude, something that was alien to our former feelings for Tanya—and that new element was keen curiosity, keen and cold like a blade of steel. . . .

"Boys! Time's up today!" said the baker one morning as he began work.

We were well aware of it without his reminder. Yet we all started.

"You watch her. . . . She'll soon come in!" suggested the baker. Some one exclaimed in a tone of regret:

"It's not a thing the eye can catch!"

And again a lively noisy argument sprang up. Today, at length, we would know how clean and incontaminate was the vessel in which we had laid all the treasure that we possessed. That morning we suddenly realized for the first time that we were gambling for high stakes, that this test of our idol might destroy it for us altogether. All these days we had been hearing that the soldier was doggedly pursuing Tanya with his attentions, but for some reason none of us asked her what her attitude was towards him. She continued regularly to call on us every morning for her pretzels and was always her usual self.

On that day, too, we soon heard her voice:

"Jail-birdies! I've come. . . ."

We hastened to let her in, and when she came in we greeted her, contrary to our custom, with silence. We looked hard at her and were at a loss what to say to her, what to ask her. We stood before her in a silent sullen crowd. She was obviously surprised at the unusual reception, and suddenly we saw her turn pale, look anxious and stir restlessly. Then in a choky voice she asked:

"Why are you all so . . . strange!"

"What about you?" threw in the baker in a grim tone, his eyes fixed on her face.

"What about me?"

"Nothing. . . ."

"Well, give me the pretzels, quick. . . ."

"Plenty of time!" retorted the baker without stirring, his eyes still glued on her face.

She suddenly turned and disappeared through the door.

The baker picked up his shovel, and turning to the oven, let fall calmly:

"Well—she's fixed! The soldier's done it . . . the blighter! . . ."

We shambled back to the table like a herd of jostling sheep, sat down in silence and apathetically set to our work. Presently some one said:

"Maybe it isn't. . . ."

"Shut up! Enough of that!" shouted the baker.

We all knew him for a clever man, cleverer than any of us. And that shout of his we understood as meaning that he was convinced of the soldier's victory. . . . We felt sad and perturbed. . . .

At twelve o'clock—the lunch hour—the soldier came in. He was, as always, clean and spruce and—as always—looked us straight in the eyes. We felt too ill at ease to look at him.

"Well, my dear sirs, d'you want me to show you what a soldier can do?" he said with a proud sneer. "You go out into the passage and peep through the cracks . . . get me?"

We trooped into the passage, and tumbling over each other, pressed our faces to the chinks in the wooden wall looking onto the yard. We did not have to wait long. Soon Tanya came through the yard with a hurried step and anxious look, skipping over puddles of thawed snow and mud. She disappeared through the door of the cellar. Presently the soldier sauntered past whistling, and he went in too. His hands were thrust into his pockets and he twitched his moustache. . . .

It was raining and we saw the drops falling into the puddles which puckered up at the impacts. It was a grey wet day—a very bleak day. Snow still lay on the roofs, while on the ground dark patches of slush stood out here and there. On the roofs too the snow was covered with a brownish coating of dirt. It was cold and disagreeable, waiting in that passage. . . .

The first to come out of the cellar was the soldier. He walked leisurely across the yard, twitching his moustache, his hands deep in his pockets—much the same as he always was.

Then Tanya came out. Her eyes . . . her eyes shone with joy and happiness, and her lips smiled. And she walked as though in a dream, swaying, with uncertain gait. . . .

It was more than we could endure. We all made a sudden rush for the door, burst into the yard and began yelling and whistling at her in a fierce, loud, savage uproar.

She started when she saw us and stood stock-still, her feet in a dirty puddle. We surrounded her and cursed her with a sort of malicious glee in a torrent of profanity and shameless taunts.

We did it unhurriedly, quietly, seeing that she had no way of escape from the circle around her and that we could jeer at her to our heart's content. It is strange, but we did not hit her. She stood amid us and turned her head from side to side, listening to our insults. And we ever more fiercely, ever more furiously, flung at her the dirt and poison of our wrath.

Her face drained of life. Her blue eyes, which the moment before had looked so happy, were dilated, her breath came in gasps and her lips quivered.

And we, having surrounded her, were wreaking our vengeance on her—for had she not robbed us? She had belonged to us, we had spent our best sentiments on her, and though that best was a mere beggar's pittance, we were twenty-six and she was one, and there was no anguish we could inflict that was fit to meet her guilt! How we insulted her! . . . She said not a word, but simply gazed at us with a look of sheer terror and a long shudder went through her body.

We guffawed, we howled, we snarled. . . . Other people joined us. . . . One of us pulled the sleeve of Tanya's blouse. . . .

Suddenly her eyes blazed; she raised her hands in a slow gesture to put her hair straight, and said loudly but calmly, straight into our faces:

"Oh, you miserable jail-birds! . . ."

And she bore straight down on us, just as if we had not been there, had not stood in her path. Indeed, that is why none of us proved to be in her path.

When she was clear of our circle she added just as loudly without turning round, in a tone of scorn and pride:

"Oh, you filthy swine. . . . You beasts. . . ." And she departed—straight, beautiful, and proud.

We were left standing in the middle of the yard amid the mud, under the rain and a grey sky that had no sun in it. . . .

Then we too shuffled back to our damp stony dungeon. As of old, the sun never peered through our window, and Tanya came never more! . . .